About Joss Wood

Joss Wood wrote her first book at the age of eight and has never really stopped. Her passion for putting letters on a blank screen is matched only by her love of books and travelling—especially to the wild places of Southern Africa—and possibly by her hatred of ironing and making school lunches.

Fuelled by coffee, when she's not writing or being a hands-on mum, Joss—with her background in business and marketing—works for a non-profit organisation to promote local economic development and the collective business interests of the area where she resides. Happily and chaotically, surrounded by books, family and friends, Joss lives in Kwa-Zulu Natal, South Africa, with her husband, children and their many pets.

TM

Wild About the Man

Joss Wood

First published in Great Britain 2013
by Mills & Boon, an imprint of Harlequin (UK) Limited.
Harlequin (UK) Limited, Eton House, 18-24 Paradise Road,
Richmond, Surrey TW9 1SR

© Joss Wood 2013

ISBN: 978 0 263 23406 0

Harlequin (UK) policy is to use papers that are natural, renewable and recyclable products and made from wood grown in sustainable forests. The logging and manufacturing process conform to the legal environmental regulations of the country of origin.

Printed and bound in Great Britain
by CPI Antony Rowe, Chippenham, Wiltshire

Also by Joss Wood

She's So Over Him

**Did you know these are also available as eBooks?
Visit www.millsandboon.co.uk**

MORAY COUNCIL LIBRARIES & INFO.SERVICES	
20 35 04 67	
Askews & Holts	
RF RF	

TM

A couple of years ago,
while sitting in a hanging basket on the edge of
Lake Malawi, after a long, lazy, sunshiny
conversation—the only type you can really have on
holiday in Malawi!—I realised that writing filled
my soul and it was time that I gave it the attention it
deserved. So for that conversation, and many, many
others around life and love, faith and hope, this book is
dedicated to our very special friends Taffy and Jen at
the Norman Carr Cottage, Namakoma Bay, Malawi.

TM

CHAPTER ONE

Luella Dawson's blog:

So, friends, my interview with Cai Campbell and Clem Copeland on my show, Night Drive with Luella last night was so much more than I—we all—expected. There was the announcement of their split—no surprise there—but what followed had us all agape. For the past ten years Cai has ducked the question of marrying Clem, so none of us expected to meet Cai's new fiancée (blonde, buxom). We were just recovering from that when he told us that he'd been shooting blanks all these years—poor Clem. Who can forget that episode of The Crazy Cs where Clem told us how her infertility was eating away at her soul?

It was early evening before Nick Sherwood made it to his desk, dusty, grumpy and sweaty. His mouth held all the moisture of the Kalahari Desert and he felt he was melting from the inside out. After grabbing a bottle of water from the small fridge behind his desk, he stood underneath the air conditioner, cracked the top of the water bottle and swallowed the contents in three big gulps. Tossing the bottle into the dustbin at his feet, he immediately opened another, resting the icy plastic against his forehead when the worst of his thirst was quenched. He'd spent most of the day in the seventeenth level of hell and the raging heat outside had only been a minor contributing factor to his nightmare day.

Normally he enjoyed taking the walking photo-safaris and it was a good way to connect with his guests; they loved the personal touch of having the owner of the six-star lodge conduct the tours. Except that he'd spent the last six hours walking so slowly that ants had dashed past them, constantly wondering when he'd have to give one of his overweight, red-faced charges CPR.

Of course they'd seen no animals, mostly because they couldn't keep their mouths shut for more than five minutes. Wildlife tended to run when confronted with loud curses, shouts and laughter.

Nick understood the animals' flight reaction; he'd considered doing the same many, many times and at various points throughout the day.

He dropped into his chair and yanked open the messy top drawer of his desk, hoping to find a container of aspirin. Eventually he found the pills and dry-swallowed three, chasing them down with the water left in the bottle in his hand.

He needed a cold beer, a swim and hot sex.

What he'd get was maintenance reports, the payroll and e-mails.

Nick pulled his computer out of standby and reached for the file on the corner of his desk. He'd barely cracked open the cover when a Skype call came in. He looked at the computer and frowned when he saw the name of his silent partner and chief investor. Hugh Copeland rarely called him and had never, in the ten years he'd known him, Skyped him.

'Good afternoon, sir.'

Copeland was at least sixty-five, formal, monstrously wealthy and Nick was still in debt to him for a couple of million. Setting up a six-star lodge wasn't cheap and maintaining a game reserve and an animal rehabilitation sanctuary sucked up money like an industrial Hoover.

Calling his chief investor 'sir' seemed appropriate.

'Nicholas. I trust you are well.' Copeland was standing, dressed in a three piece suit. When he placed his arms on the back of his chair and glared into the camera Nick caught a hint of a flashing temper in his light grape-green eyes.

Trouble. Nick cursed. And it was heading straight for him.

'Very, sir. What can I do for you?' he asked as his heart raced. He'd submitted his financial report to his office, paid the instalment—and more—on his loan… What else could he have done to earn this man's displeasure? Copeland had a twenty-five per cent stake in his company and he mostly left Nick alone.

'I've been trying to contact you since this morning.'

Hell.

'I was on a walking safari, I've just got in.' Nick decided to bite the bullet and get it over with. 'What's the problem and how can I fix it?'

'I am sending Clementine to you.'

Clementine? Who was Clementine? Nick shook his head. 'Who?'

'My daughter, Nicholas. She's landed herself in a spot of bother and needs a place to escape to. Somewhere private and isolated and remote.'

Nick lifted dark eyebrows. 'What type of trouble?'

If she'd murdered someone or needed rehab, he'd rather not take her, millions owing or not.

He'd rather not take her, period.

'Press trouble. They want her blood. Her common law husband of a decade introduced her to his new fiancée on a nationally syndicated television chat show.'

Nick worked through that, and then winced in sympathy. Ouch. He searched his memory bank and recalled that his partner had a daughter living with Cai Campbell who, in his opinion, was a mediocre musician at best.

And what was with all the names starting with the letter C? Clem, Cai. Copeland. Campbell.

Nick snorted. Typical Hollywood. There were another twenty-five letters in the alphabet.

So Campbell dumped his ex-model partner for a newer version...and she was now his problem. In what universe was that fair?

'She's coming here?'

Copeland must have heard the doubt in his voice because his gaze sharpened. 'Is that a problem?'

Nick folded his arms and nodded. 'Actually, sir, yes, it is. We're one of a handful of six-star lodges in Africa and we're booked up to a year in advance. We do not have any vacancies and my next opening is next year.'

She can come back then, Nick thought. And she, like everyone else, could pay for the privilege.

The old man cursed, rather eloquently, Nick thought. 'You have nothing at all?'

'Two dormitory-style beds in a room in the junior rangers' house.'

Those piercing eyes narrowed. 'Don't you have a spare room in your house?'

Hell, no!

'Uh—'

'Well?'

'I don't think my house is up to her standards. I mean, it's OK, but not like the rooms in the Lodge.'

'She'll cope. And if she doesn't, then she can just deal with it.'

Nick closed his eyes and counted to ten. He opened his eyes to see that Copeland was now sitting on the corner of his desk. He stared at Nick and tapped his finger against his thigh. Nick didn't need him to voice the obvious:

Ten years ago I was the one person prepared to listen to a twenty-five-year lunatic who had nothing more than a Masters degree in Zoology, the shirt on his back and a piece of land adjoining the Kruger National Park. I took a chance on you... You owe me.

Nick sighed. Message received, loud and clear. 'When does she arrive?'

Copeland looked at his slim watch. 'In about thirty minutes; she's flying in on my jet into your airfield.'

Oh, so he'd never really had the option of saying no.

'Fine.' It wasn't but what could he do?

'Thank you, Nicholas. I do appreciate this.'

Nick tipped his head back to look at the ceiling above his head. What had he done that warranted him being sentenced to sharing his house with a society princess—born with not a silver spoon but a canteen of diamond encrusted cutlery in her mouth—and who had a doctorate in being a rich man's arm candy?

He rested his forehead on his desk. All he wanted was a cold beer, a swim and sex. Really, was that too much to ask?

In her father's jet, Clem Copeland yawned, stretched and blinked away the last remnants of a brief restless sleep. She tucked her long legs up under her and caught the eye of her best friend, and personal assistant, who sat in the chair opposite her, eyeing her with quiet sympathy. Jason had been with her since her modelling days and he knew her inside out and upside down. As the memories of the past thirty-six hours rushed back to pummel her, she was grateful for his shoulder to lean on.

Tears, hot and angry, fell.

'Sweetheart.' Jason sighed, handed her a bottle of water and patted her knee.

'It wasn't just a horrible dream, was it?'

'Sorry.' Jason pursed his lips and shook his head. 'Selfish, narcissistic ass.'

Clem saluted him with her bottle. 'Careful, Jace, or else I'll start to think that you don't like him.'

'I've never liked him! And I told you that he was planning something.' Jason shoved both hands into his bleached blond hair, visibly frustrated.

'I thought that if we could part amicably, then the press would shrug it off. After all, they've been predicting our breakup for years!' Clem protested.

'Cai has all the morals of an alley cat. He's lied to you for ten years and yet you still fall for it!' Jason poured himself a glass of wine and downed the contents in one long swallow. Clem reached for a tissue and wiped her eyes, light green and surrounded by long tinted lashes. Wet from her tears, they were even more startling than normal. 'I'm *not* crying because I'm sad, I always cry when I'm angry!'

'Mmm.'

'I swear this time I could just boil him in oil.' Clem gripped the bridge of her nose. 'How long do you think he's known her for and when did he propose? Two weeks? Three? That was quite a ring he'd bought her.'

'You're avoiding the subject.'

Damn right she was. That Cai had announced their breakup and introduced the world to her replacement and had proposed to her was humiliating enough, but the other bombshell he'd oh-so-casually dropped rearranged every atom in her body.

'At least I vomited into her designer tote. That had to be a highlight.'

'On national TV. But you did hide most of your face in her bag so you did it very discreetly.'

'Thanks for pulling me off the show during that commercial break.'

'Yeah. I've never hit anyone in my life but I came close to decking him.'

Clem tried to smile but her lips refused to co-operate. She dropped her legs and rested her forearms on her knees. She stared at the plush carpet beneath her knee length boots. When she looked up, she saw Jason's occasional grimace as he worked on his laptop.

'I've accessed the onboard Internet service,' he explained.

'I figured. How big is the fallout?' Clem asked in a dull voice.

'Nuclear.'

Clem ran her hand over her eyes. 'Let me guess what the headlines say… "What would Roz think?" or "Clem is not a chip off the old block" or "Was Clem swapped at birth"?'

Jason sighed. 'Not quite so harsh but getting there.'

'Can I not just have my own little public meltdown without them bringing in my mother?'

Jason pursed his lips. 'If your mother had been anyone else, maybe.' Anyone other than a glamorous heavyweight war correspondent and news presenter, public darling, rising political star and tipped to be the future prime minister. 'But you know that the press have hyper-idealised her since she died in her prime.'

'And I've lived down to her memory.' Clem pushed her waist length hair over her shoulder and held the large ornate silver locket that hung from her neck on a heavy silver chain.

'You've just taken a different path to her,' Jason said quietly.

'I took a different motorway as fast and as hard as I could.'

Jason draped one plump leg over the other and linked his hands around his knee. 'You once told me that you had a hole inside you before she died, that all you wanted was her time and she was always so busy. Do you think you used Cai to fill up that hole?'

'No, I fell into bed with Cai in a rush of hormones because I was nineteen and stupid,' Clem replied, her voice tart in response to his prodding. She was coming off a bad breakup and Jason wanted to analyse her relationship with her dead mother? Not going to happen. 'He was hot, older and I loved his rock and roll lifestyle. And, I repeat, because I was nineteen and stupid. You shouldn't make life changing decisions when you are nineteen.'

'Or, obviously, when you are stupid,' Jason added.

Clem sighed. She should've just cut her losses nine years and six months ago. Then she wouldn't be sitting in her father's jet, running from the press and feeling as if she was about to snap under the weight of this soul scorching rage.

Clem sat back and folded her arms. 'Where are we going by the way? We've been flying for ever. The villa in the Seychelles? The flat in Sydney?'

Jason shook his head. 'Your father is sending you to a private game reserve in South Africa.'

Clem's arched eyebrows flew up. 'You've got to be joking! Africa? Animals? Insects? Sun? I'm a redhead, for goodness' sake!'

Jason smiled. 'Sorry, honey, but we did ask for private and isolated. The press are going to try and track you wherever you go and they won't find you there. It's a very exclusive, very expensive lodge. One of those where you pay a set price and everything is included, including spa treatments. They have elephant-back safaris—you should do that.'

Clem narrowed her eyes at him. 'Uh...no! Can you see me riding high in the blistering sun, going "Oooh! There's a buck" or "Wow! There's another"?'

'You should open yourself up to new experiences.'

'I don't do the country or anything close to it!' Clem stared out of the window. 'We'll just have to make the best of it.'

'You'll have to make the best of it,' Jason corrected and shrugged when her eyes connected with his. 'The Baobab and Buffalo Lodge has a bed for you but not me. I'm going home with the plane.'

'But I need you!'

'I need to go back to do damage control. You know I do.'

Clem tapped her fingers against her thigh, thinking of an argument to keep him with her. She wasn't joking when she said she needed him; she didn't want to be alone.

Her heart contracted and her throat closed again. She bit her lip so hard that her teeth left marks in the skin.

'You know, I get that I'm spoilt and lazy, selfish and inconsiderate.' Jason started to protest but the small shake of her head had the words dying on his lips. Clem shrugged. 'I have too much time and money and I've done a lot of things I'm not proud of. I don't love Cai any more and he's welcome to get married... Seriously, I wish her luck.'

'But?'

'He knew how much I wanted a child, Jace. So why would he let me think that I was infertile for so long? He came with me when I went for all those tests, took my temperature to check if I was ovulating, slept with me—well, up until a year or so ago—when the time was right. He did all that, all the while knowing that he had a vasectomy before we even met! Why would he do that?'

'Because he's a jerk who likes to play games?'

'That would explain it.' Clem sniffed and blew her nose. 'I think we're banking, we must be nearly there.'

'Then maybe you should fix your face,' Jason suggested. 'You look like hell, you know, from all your *angry* tears.'

Next to the runway, Nick sat on the bonnet of his roofless Land Rover. His scarred boots rested on the bull bar and he watched the blood-red sun sink behind the bank of acacia trees. It was his favourite time of day and the heat was holding steady. He looked at the cloudless sky and sighed. The daily temperatures were climbing towards unbearable, the waterholes were almost dry and the residents, human, bird and animal, were desperate for the first of the summer rains, which had yet to arrive.

But sunsets like these were one of the myriad reasons why he'd worked sixteen, eighteen-hour days for the best part of a decade. He considered it a privilege to watch the sun go down and listen to the night song of a little piece of Africa that was under his protection.

From his first memory of walking this land with his paternal grandfather at the age of four, he'd felt an affinity for this place, this soil. He loved the element of danger, the age old fight of the survival of the fittest. Two-B had always been his sanctuary, his favourite place in the world, the place that fed his soul. As a child he'd run to his grandfather and this land when being the only introvert in a large family of noisy, outspoken, non-privacy-respecting, intimacy-demanding party animals became overwhelming. He'd find the peace and solitude here he needed and never found in his chaotic family home, surrounded by four siblings and left-of-centre parents. He could never imagine living or working anywhere else.

After university, because he was used to being the best, he'd gone big, aiming to establish a six-star lodge—exclusive, expensive, elitist. Finding an investor had been a hassle but his father's old school tie network had come in handy and his parent had browbeaten his school buddy Copeland into meeting with him. He'd walked away with thirty million in his pocket and minus a twenty-five per cent share of his company.

It had been a good day.

Working his dream of creating one of the premier game reserves in Africa had meant sacrifices: time, money, a social life. His need for stability and...serenity...had led him into a five-year marriage which, ultimately, resulted in him being estranged from his family.

Choices and consequences were a bitch.

But his wife was long gone and he was content being single. Besides it was, Nick decided, too much of a fag to look for a woman who could, firstly, tolerate living in isolation and then would be prepared to live with a man who'd made the conscious decision to remain emotionally unavailable.

Essentially, he wanted a witty conversationalist with superior mattress skills who'd be happy to be ignored as and when he pleased.

Unfortunately, he'd hadn't yet heard where those aliens had landed.

Brief affairs, he'd stick to those. Tidier, easier, less complicated…and not difficult to find when he felt the woman was interesting enough to make the effort.

He rubbed his hand over his face. Where had all these thoughts about love and life come from? Must have been triggered by hearing that Copeland's daughter had come an emotional cropper…

Nick heard the distinctive sound of turbine engines and picked up his hand held radio. He glanced down the runway to check that it was still empty—it wasn't uncommon to see lions stretched out on the tar or impala nibbling at the grass on the edges. He tuned into the open frequency and informed the pilots that they were good to land. The plane rushed past him and he stayed were he was, watching as it slowed, turned at the bottom of the strip and taxied back up the runway towards him. The door opened and the co-pilot dropped the stairs and jogged down, holding out a hand for Nick to shake.

'Nice landing,' Nick said, jamming his hands into his khaki shorts.

'Thanks.' He looked around. 'Wow, seriously wild. So, no lions, huh?'

'Not today.' Nick turned and looked up as a figure appeared in the doorway of the cabin. Her hair was a long fall of pale rust, several shades lighter than his wife's fire-red, shot through with strawberry-blonde streaks that even the most expensive salon could not recreate. Sculpted cheekbones, a pixie chin and a body that was long, lean and scrawny.

'Jace, I'm going to miss you. Thank you.'

'Keep in touch. You will get through this.' The voice was deep and rumbling.

'Call me when you get home.'

The words floated down to Nick and her voice was low, melodious and as smooth as syrup. English, with the slightest crisp that good schooling added. She sauntered—he doubted this woman knew the meaning of the word walk—down the steps dressed in a white man's style shirt, a strip of fabric across her hips that might, when it grew up, become a skirt, solid black tights and knee length boots. She looked like every one of the several million dollars she was reputed to be worth. Then he noticed her father's eyes, the colour of seedless green grapes, and forgot how to breathe. Long lashes and arched brows framed them to perfection.

He'd been fired on by poachers, faced down a charging elephant and had an engine out in his Cessna but his lungs had never just stopped working like this before. Breathe, you idiot, he told himself, before you pass out at her feet.

Nick sucked in a hot, deep breath, needing the air to smooth out his bumping breath, his racing heart. While his wife had been all banked flames and controlled heat, he suspected this one was a raging bush fire.

Lord, another redhead. Like malaria, buffaloes and black mambas, experience had taught him that they were best avoided.

Three things slapped Clem simultaneously as she stepped out of the plane. It was scorchingly hot, it was desperately wild and she was totally out of her depth.

She wanted to go home.

She nearly turned around, opened her mouth to tell Jason that she was returning with him, when she saw him standing on the tarmac, looking up at her. For the first time—ever—she forgot what she'd been about to say.

Nut-brown hair, overlong and shaggy, topped a face that

was as rugged as the land surrounding them. Light stubble, thin lips and can't-BS-me—grey? green?—eyes. He was tall—six two, six three—and built. A swimmer's body, she decided, her eyes tracing his broad shoulders and slim hips. It was easy to imagine his rippled stomach, the long muscles in his thighs.

Her earlier description of the land applied to him as well. Scorchingly hot and desperately wild.

Clem caught the intelligence in his eyes and the wry twist of his lips told her that he'd already made up his mind about her. Spoilt, snobby, stuck up. The hell of it was that he was right, she was all of those things and, oh, damn...she instinctively knew she couldn't play him, couldn't charm him, couldn't snow him. And she, especially, didn't like being summed up so quickly, and so well.

He angled his head when she reached the bottom of the stairs. She noticed, and was glad, that he didn't hold out his hand for her to shake. 'Ms Copeland, I'm Nick Sherwood.'

His voice was moderately deep and held more of an English accent than she'd expected. It sent a shiver skittering along her spine and she frowned... What on earth was wrong with her?

Clem watched as he shot a glance at Joe, who was transferring her luggage from the hold onto the back seat of what she thought might have once been a Land Rover, checked his watch and tapped his foot. He couldn't have made it clearer that she was an imposition and a waste of his precious time.

Really, who did he think he was? King of all he surveyed? He was very confident—almost insolent—for an employee. Pity that impertinence came wrapped up in such a smoking hot package.

'Aren't you going to help him?' she demanded.

Nick looked at Joe, looked back at her and shook his head. 'He's got it under control.'

Grrr. Clem fanned her face and plucked her white shirt

off her overheated skin. 'I'm so hot I could die. Is it always this hot?'

'It's Africa. Spring going into summer. It's hot but it helps if you're appropriately dressed. Shorts and T-shirts, yes. Tights and boots, no.'

'Get me some water...' Clem started to say please and sneezed instead. She watched his eyes narrow and she knew that he didn't like spoilt, annoying, demanding women. Well, that suited her just fine because she didn't like the fact that he made her skin prickle and...

'No.' Nick pointed at the plane. 'Feel free to climb the stairs and get it yourself.'

Clem shrugged and called up the stairs. 'Jace? Please ask Chloe for a bottle of water for me, I'm melting.'

'So, you do have a vague concept of what passes for rudimentary manners,' Nick commented.

Jason appeared at the top of the stairs, a bottle of water in his hand. He scooted down the stairs, handed it to Clem and sent Nick a sympathetic smile as he shook his hand and introduced himself. 'Clem's always impossible when she's in a mood.'

'I am not in a mood.' Clem stamped her boot and dust billowed. She coughed and waved it away. 'And if I were, I'm entitled!'

'Not around me you're not,' Sherwood stated.

'You are exceptionally rude.'

'Ditto.'

Clem gestured to his vehicle with her over-sized glasses. It was more rust than paint and looked about fifty years old.

'So, I suppose that's your vehicle?'

'It is.'

Huh. Mr Talkative he was not. Normally, most men would be falling over by now, chatting her up, fluffing their feathers. He just stood there, looking sexy. And hot. And annoyed.

Clem twisted the top of her bottle of water but the top held firm. After a couple more tries, Nick took the bottle, cracked the lid in one try and handed it back to her.

'Thank you.'

Nick smirked, which made Clem just want to poke him. 'So, is it your job to pick up guests?'

'Sometimes.'

'And does your boss know you're picking up guests in a battered, rusty car that looks like it's about to fall apart? It's not the right image for a luxury lodge.'

Nick narrowed his eyes and folded his arms. The veins in his forearms raised his skin and she swallowed. She'd always found that physical indication of fitness sexy.

'No, the guests are normally collected in the game viewing vehicles but they are all being used at the moment.'

'It's six in the evening. What are they being used for at this time of night?'

'Oh, let's think. We're on a game reserve. What would game vehicles be used for...? Um, maybe game viewing?'

Oh, could she sound any more stupid if she tried? Clem winced, looked down and kicked a loose stone with the toe of her boot. 'There's no need to be sarcastic,' she muttered.

'I haven't even reached sarcastic yet.'

Ooh, fighting talk. Clem snapped her head up. 'Do you talk to all the guests like this?'

'Not usually.'

'So, why do I get your special treatment?'

Nick stepped over to the Land Rover and yanked open the passenger door, ignoring the fact that the door was attached with just one hinge. 'You're not a guest. You're me doing your father a favour. Get in.'

'I don't understand what you're muttering about and my father won't like your attitude. So check it or I will have you fired.'

Clem caught the light roll of his eyes and realized that this man wasn't in the least bit fazed by her unusually sharp tongue and simmering temper. She looked into his cool grey eyes and saw that he didn't give a flying fig for what she thought.

While she didn't like him, her respect for him soared. When last had she met a man with a healthy ego?

'Your father is old friends with my attitude and, unlike you, knows exactly how far he can push me. And, since I own The Baobab and Buffalo Lodge, your threats are both childish and unnecessary,' Nick said in a cool, calm, measured tone. The lack of temper in his voice made her feel about two feet high.

Was she ever going to win a round with this tall, rangy, *muscly,* grey-eyed demon?

'Are you going to get your butt into the Landy or are you going to walk?' His voice had fallen to sub-zero and she wished she could step inside it and cool down. She was quite certain there was a lake of perspiration in her boots.

Clem ignored the hand he held out, looked at the vehicle and bit her lip. Her skirt was too tight and too short for her to step up onto the runner board. She needed to bend her leg to step up and if she did that, then the Odious Owner and the pilot would get a great view of her tights covered bottom.

Clem cursed, looked at the runner board again and scratched her head.

'Problem, Red?'

He needed to visit charm school, Clem fumed. She turned to face him and because she was so tall—five foot seven without heels—she just needed to lift her eyes to connect with his. She was annoyed to find that she had to swallow the excess saliva in her mouth. Good grief, she'd met some of the best looking men in the world and none of them made her mouth water. The last time she'd had such a physical re-action was when she'd first seen Cai and look how well that had turned out.

Not.

You're tired, upset and emotional. Nothing has been normal about this day, the last couple of days, she reminded herself. Nothing had been normal about the last ten years.

Besides, any man would look good after what Cai did and said to you. Add it to the fact that she hadn't had sex for close to a year and...whoosh! Chemical reaction.

'We're wasting daylight here,' Nick snapped and Clem rubbed her forehead, trying to focus.

'I can't,' she said. 'Not without embarrassing myself and you. And Joe.'

'What are you going on about?'

Clem dropped her hands and pointed to the hem of her skirt. 'It's too tight and too short. I can't lift my leg to get up without flashing.'

Nick rubbed his hand down his face and Clem was pretty sure it was to cover his grin. She glared at him. 'It's not funny.'

'Judging by the number of naked photos there are of you in cyberspace, I'm surprised at your modesty.'

'Now, you're the one being stupid. Haven't you heard of Photoshop? Every one of those images out there is my head on someone else's body.'

Instead of looking chastised, Nick grinned and Clem felt as if she'd taken another mental body blow. It transformed his tough face from attractive to mind-blowingly, panty-scrunchingly, take-me-to-bed attractive.

Oh no! No, no, no, no.

While she was trying to get her dancing hormones under control, Nick slid a hand around her back, the other under her thighs, scooped her up and, in one easy and fluid movement, dumped her in the passenger seat of the vehicle. She had an impression of effortless strength, a hard chest, a spicy scent.

Then her bottom hit an exposed spring in the seat and she yelped.

'Oh, and mind the spring,' Nick suggested as he walked

around the car, hopped onto the runner board and stepped over the closed door to drop into the driver's seat.

Clem sat on one buttock and rubbed the other. 'You did that on purpose!' she accused.

'Now we both have a pain in our butt,' Nick commented and sent her a smile that any shark would be proud of.

'I really don't like you.'

'Back at you,' Nick muttered. 'Now, can we get out of here? I want a shower and a beer.'

Clem leaned over the door and held out her hand to Joe, the co-pilot. 'Thank you. Tell Nathan and Chloe I say thank you as well. Safe flight.'

Joe didn't have much time to respond before Nick floored the vehicle and pulled away.

Clem held onto her seat and closed her eyes.

Ho, ho, ho, ho…it's off to another part of hell I go.

CHAPTER TWO

Luella Dawson's blog:

While fans of the reality TV show The Crazy Cs weren't surprised at their decision to separate, they were shocked by Cai's method of announcing it to the world. Public sympathy is lying with Clem and fans are clamouring for more footage of the couple now that the last of the series has just been aired. Campbell has responded by agreeing to do another ten episodes of the reality show but insiders know it will mean little without Clem's side of the story. So where is the flamboyant heiress and ex-model? That, readers, is the million dollar question. Wherever she is, we're presuming that she's not having fun.

AFTER ten minutes of silence, Nick looked across at his passenger and noticed that the pale hand clutching the heavy silver locket was white in the setting sun. Tendrils of that, admittedly, amazing hair had escaped from the messy knot she'd pulled it into and were dancing in the wind. Her bottom lip remained between her teeth.

He could have been more welcoming, he supposed, but he'd been side-winded by the X-rated flashes of what he wanted to do to her in bed. Or he had been until she'd opened her mouth and starting spewing Diva. He'd had major royalty and minor royalty staying at the Lodge, movie stars and moguls, but she'd out prima donna-ed them all.

Nick glanced down at those long legs and thought that she could do with a couple of cheeseburgers. She was tall but too thin, her face held that pinched look that women got when they'd lived on a diet of lettuce and multi-vitamins for far too many years. He recognized the type. A lot of the trophy wives or girlfriends who glided in and out of the Lodge had the same look—sucked-in cheeks, stick-thin legs, silicone-enhanced breasts.

He dropped his eyes to her chest. He'd bet hers were natural—small, round... He shifted in his seat. If he was getting horny thinking about this skinny wildcat then he definitely needed to get some action soon.

Nick rubbed the back of his neck, saw the long, drooping branch of a thorn tree and spoke for the first time in ten minutes. 'Mind the branch.'

Naturally, she didn't listen and a long thorn caught her shirt, ripped through the fabric and scratched her skin. She squealed, looked down at her arm and squealed again.

Nick sent her a cursory glance and carried on driving. 'Hell, woman, it's just a scratch!'

'There are drops of blood, it stings and this is a designer shirt! It's torn!'

'Call the fashion police; maybe they'll care,' Nick retorted. 'Next time I say "mind the branch" I suggest you mind the branch.'

'Aaargh! I hate this place and your stupid thorn trees and the heat and you!' Clem yelled. Nick responded by deliberately hitting a bump in the dirt road and she bounced in the seat. He smiled.

'And I hate this sodding seat with its stupid broken spring!'

Nick saw the twin flags of anger in her cheeks and her wobbling chin and erred on the side of caution and didn't respond. He didn't want to get brained with the oversized bag that sat on her lap. It looked heavy. He swung the Land Rover onto the road to the Lodge, sparing a glance at the pair of giraffes nibbling on an acacia tree.

'Evening, boys.' He frequently spoke to the animals he came across and didn't care if his guests thought he was nuts. He glanced across at Clem and noticed that she still had that thousand yard stare.

'Giraffe to your left.'

Clem didn't respond and Nick shrugged. He caught the swish of a tail out of the corner of his eye, braked and reversed.

She stood with her monstrous back to them, a tiny calf at her heels... A week, ten days old, Nick surmised, craning his head to see if he could identify the female elephant. But she kept her face stubbornly hidden and Nick eventually pulled off.

'Her calf is very young; the rest of the nursery herd should be around here somewhere,' Nick said as they climbed the last hill to the Lodge. Through the dusky, dusty air, he could see the blazing lights of the Lodge and the staff village beyond.

Clem turned to look at him. 'What are you talking about?'

Nick frowned. 'The elephant and her calf.' She looked blank. 'The one that was a couple of metres from you?'

'I didn't see it,' Clem said tonelessly.

Nick cursed, slammed on the brakes, put the car in neutral, reached across her lap and yanked open the door to the cubbyhole. Scratching around, his hand closed around the small torch and he flicked the switch. Grabbing Clem's chin, he shone the light into her eyes.

She slapped his hand away but Nick persevered. 'What are you doing?'

'Are you on drugs?' Nick demanded. Her pupils looked normal but what did he know?

Clem yanked the torch from his hand and threw it onto

the floor at her feet. 'No, I'm not on drugs! Why would you think that?'

'Because there was a four-ton elephant right next to you and you didn't notice!' Nick shouted.

She turned to look behind her. 'Oh. Where?'

Nick muttered a curse and rested his forehead on his wrists, his hands gripping the wheel to keep them from encircling her neck. When the urge to throw her into the nearest bush passed, he put the Landy in gear and drove through the decorative gates that marked the gateway to the Lodge.

Give me strength, he begged. She was worse than he'd imagined.

Although it was not completely dark yet, lights blazed from the two-storey Edwardian villa that had once been his great-great-grandfather's hunting 'cottage'. Built in grey stone, the house sported an imposing portico over marble steps and Nick pulled up behind the four game viewing vehicles that were offloading guests. Two of his butlers were on hand to distribute glasses of sherry to the guests and he caught the babble of excited voices. Unlike his passenger, they were excited about what they'd seen in the bush.

Jumping out of his car, Nick headed for his head ranger and spoke to him in fluent Shangaan. 'All well?'

Jabu's white teeth gleamed in his dark face. '*Mfo.*' He used the shortened but still traditional greeting for brother and friend—*mfowethu*—and they were. They'd grown up together and Jabu was his right-hand man, more partner than employee.

'Who's the woman?' Jabu asked him after they'd had a quick discussion about the morning's schedule. He glanced at Clem, who was looking up at the Lodge with what he thought might be approval in her eyes.

'Copeland's daughter. She's staying with me at the house.'

Jabu's brown eyes danced. 'Been telling you that you need a woman, *mfo*. Try to last more than a minute.'

'Funny.' Nick scowled. 'I'd rather mate with a honey badger. She needs a severe attitude adjustment.'

'Can't help noticing that she's a redhead,' Jabu said with a sly grin.

'Yeah, but so are fire ants.' Nick slapped Jabu's shoulder and walked back towards his vehicle, tossing his next sentence over his shoulder. 'I'll see you boys in The Pit later, you can buy me a beer.'

The Pit was the staff bar which adjoined the staff games rooms, where the rangers and staff working at the Lodge and the animal sanctuary could, in addition to the gym, TV room and a computer gaming room, chill out after a long day.

Nick took a moment to look at the Lodge and sighed with pleasure. The deep green grass complemented the double storey grey-blue stone house and carefully landscaped indigenous gardens added to the luxurious feel. No matter the time of day, the house always looked welcoming, the staff were, without fail, convivial and helpful and his guests stepped into unparalleled luxury.

He frequently wished he could have the guests' money without having the guests but the unfortunate reality was that he needed his top dollar clients to fund the running of the reserve.

Nick heard a loud whooping sound and smiled when he heard his chief butler, Simon, reassuring a nervous guest that the hyena laughing was definitely behind the electric fence. The Lodge, the staff village and the animal sanctuary all had a perimeter electric fence to ensure that his guests, staff and wounded animals didn't become a snack for a prowling leopard or stalking lion. His own house was situated outside the security fence, closer to the edge of the cliff and away from the Lodge.

It was his refuge, his safe haven, his favourite place in the world. Or it had been until Princess Red's arrival.

Clem stood up in her seat and Nick raised an eyebrow at her when he reached the Landy. 'And now?'

'If you'd be so kind as to help me down and show me to my room, we can say goodnight and maybe try to be civil to each other when next we meet.'

Oh, that cool voice just killed him. It immediately made him want to rattle her cage. 'You think you're staying here?'

'Aren't I?'

Nick hopped back in the vehicle. 'Not unless you booked a room approximately a year to eighteen months ago. Did you?'

'Stop being facetious and tell me where I'm sleeping!' Clem retorted, those incredible eyes flashing. She reminded him of a snapping turtle he'd once seen in Florida—mean, ornery and...snappy.

'You're sleeping with me, Red. In my house but not in my bed, just in case you have any ideas to the contrary.'

'I'd rather sleep with my ex. And if you could measure how much I detest him right now, then you'd realise how monstrous an insult that is.'

Two nights later Clem sat, Indian style, on her bed under the mosquito net in Nick's guest room, her open book unread in her lap. She hadn't ventured further than his kitchen in two days and the last real conversation she'd had, with anyone, was the clipped one she'd exchanged with Nick the night he'd shown her to this room. In fact, it wasn't a conversation, it was more Nick throwing a couple of orders at her head.

There was food and drink in the fridge; she had to help herself. If she left anything out in the outdoor shower, the monkeys or baboons would probably swipe it, especially if it sparkled. If she saw a snake, stand still. Sleep under the mozzie net; this was malaria country. She shouldn't walk around outside because the electric fence didn't extend to his house and if she heard any noises outside, she shouldn't investigate. It could be a lion, leopard, hyena, all of which would like to take a chunk of her skinny hide.

Clem rested her head on her bent knees, grateful for the swirl of cool air from the air conditioner. She felt utterly drained, as if someone had taken her and wiped the floor with her head. She'd held herself together until she'd heard Nick leaving in that wretched vehicle the night before last and then she'd dissolved. She'd sobbed for hours and hours and when she'd heard him returning she'd buried her head under her pillow and cried some more.

Utterly drained, she knew that the worst of the emotional storm had passed and, as it passed, a modicum of sanity returned.

It would be so much less embarrassing if she could say that she was crying over the loss of a grand passion, a soulmate, her raison d'être. But she couldn't because she'd meant what she said on the plane about Cai—she didn't care if he married what's-her-face or an alien. Every last emotion she'd felt for him was dead, six feet under, and she just wanted to get past him and onto the rest of her life.

So that couldn't explain why she'd spent the last two days raising the world's water levels.

Clem buried the heels of her hands into her eye sockets and whimpered. The truth she could no longer avoid was that she was crying over lost time, stupid decisions, wasted years, humiliation, embarrassment and, hardest of all to admit, brazen, in your face and utterly fearless...fear.

Terror.

For the second time in her life the foundations of her world had been washed away. When her mother died she'd been rocked to her core. Nothing in the world made sense until Cai came along with his 'live for today' philosophy. He'd encouraged her to pursue instant gratification and the pursuit of pleasure had ruled their lives.

At the time it had made sense to her.

Fast forward a decade and what had she to show for those decisions? A spectacularly public failed mock-marriage, a closet full of clothes and an identity that was wrapped up in being Roz Hedley-Copeland's daughter and Cai Campbell's lover.

If only she'd had the brains, the confidence to kick him to touch after she'd found out about his first affair but he'd talked her out of it. Guilted her out of it as well.

No, don't study...you're too pretty to put your nose into a book.

A job? Why would anyone want to hire a washed up ex-model who has never worked a day in her life?

Working for charity? You?

Face it, darling, you're not much good for anything more difficult than looking gorgeous.

Puke.

So what could she do, who was she going to be? She needed to find a new normal, a new reality, a new everything and she was scared, soul-deep terrified.

Clem rolled over in bed and placed her forearm over her eyes. She couldn't hide out in a stranger's house in South Africa for ever but the thought of leaving had the breath catching in her throat, her heart pounding. She couldn't leave until the press furore died down, and until she had some sort of plan... She couldn't face her father, the press, the world without one.

Or that grey-eyed, six foot something of bolshie attitude on the other side of her door.

The thing was, she'd never had to do this on her own before and she didn't know where to start.

Jabu had met Nick after the evening game drive and accepted Nick's offer of a beer back at his house. Nick dumped his radio on the long wooden dining table while Jabu yanked two beers out of his fridge and cracked the tops. The door to his guest's bedroom was still firmly shut and Nick frowned at the half-eaten tub of yoghurt and the barely touched apple on a plate next to the sink.

He was going to have to do something about the redhead soon but he had no idea what.

Jabu handed him a beer and walked from the kitchen to the lounge, sliding open the doors that led onto the deck. His house was a rectangle, with the well designed kitchen, study and a home gym at the back of the house. The kitchen, dining room and lounge were all open-plan, with a long wooden table covered in books, files and rolled up maps separating the leather couches of the lounge from the kitchen counters. A flat-screen TV with an X-box attached dominated the wall and floor-to-ceiling wood and glass sliding doors led out onto the wooden deck.

It was comfortable and he liked it—a far cry from the two room shack he and Terra had shared in the early days.

Nick followed Jabu out to the deck and imitated his friend's stance, forearms on the railing, beer bottle dangling from two fingers as they scanned the vegetation below. A herd of zebra were grazing to the right, impala were in the thick bush a little way away.

'We need to move those rhinos we bought from up north,' Jabu commented.

'The translocation costs a freaking bomb. The Foundation doesn't have the cash right now to fund it. The charity ball is in a month's time, though…I'm hoping for some big donations to come in then. Can we wait that long?'

'We can but I don't know about the rhinos.' Jabu sipped his beer and sent Nick a sly look. 'How's your guest?'

Nick shrugged. 'Dunno. Haven't seen her. She stays in her room.'

Jabu's eyebrows lifted. 'For two days?'

'Hey, it suits me. She has an attitude that can strip paint off walls.' Nick blew out his breath. 'I don't know what to do about her. She was a royal pain when she stepped off the plane but I can cope with that. But she's shut herself in her room and doesn't come out when I'm here. She's not eating, she's not sleeping. I hear her pacing.' Nick took a pull of his beer. 'I keep thinking that I should make her work, which is just crazy.'

'Why?'

'I doubt she's worked a day in her life. But I keep remembering what your mother said to me when Terra…you know. That work is the best medicine.'

'My mama is a wise woman. Crazy mad but wise. I think you're right. Get her out of that room and interacting with people.' Jabu pushed off the railing. 'I must go…I need to spend some time with the kids before bed.' He took Nick's empty bottle and shook his head when Nick started to accompany him out. 'Stay here. Decide what you want to do about Clem. Later.'

'Night, Jabs.'

Nick returned back to his previous stance and looked down the steep cliff at a chattering dove on a rock halfway down the cliff. The zebras had moved off and a jackal scurried across the bank of the waterhole. The sun dropped behind the thorn trees and the subdued gold between the branches was the same shade as Clem's hair.

He was tired of living with a ghoul. Like it or not, Clem was going to work.

It felt as if Clem had just drifted off to sleep when Nick yanked back the heavy curtains and bright morning sunlight streamed over her bed and into her eyes. She yelped and covered her eyes as he banged a cup of coffee on the night stand next to her.

'Coffee,' Nick told her. 'Get up, Princess.'

Clem groaned and when her eyes focused on the bedside clock she growled, 'It's five o'clock in the morning.'

'Yeah, and you're going to be late. Get moving, Red.' Nick

grabbed her mosquito net, spun it and expertly tied it into a knot. He yanked back her sheet and stared down at her long body, barely covered by a tight cotton camisole and low-slung cotton sleeping shorts. The shirt had ridden up to reveal four inches of her flat stomach, complete with a diamond stud in her belly button. Nick immediately wanted to dip his tongue there, feel the contrast between the cool stone and her warm skin.

Clem half sat and glared up at him, pushing her riotous hair back with her hand. 'What is wrong with you?'

Nick backed away from the bed and placed his fists on khaki-covered hips. 'Your free ride at Two-B—what we call The Baobab and Buffalo Lodge—is over. You can wallow while you work.'

'I have no idea what you are talking about.' Clem sat up properly and immediately reached for the cup of coffee. She took a sip and closed her eyes in appreciation.

'You're going to get out of bed and do some work,' Nick told her, thinking that he had to get out of her room before he put her to work in a very different, and far more pleasurable, way. He kept seeing places on her body, apart from the obvious, he wanted to explore. A spot on her foot underneath the fine ankle chain, the pulse point at the bottom of her throat, the place where her jaw met her neck that looked so soft, so silky.

Nick hovered by the door. 'You've got fifteen minutes. We leave then, however you're dressed.'

Clem stared at him as if he'd lost his mind. 'No! You're not the boss of me!'

'How old are you? Five?' Nick stalked back to the bed, hiding the fact that he was pleased to see some fire in her eyes, heat in her cheeks. 'And, actually, I am. This is my house, my property, my business. In case you haven't noticed, you are sleeping in my bed, drinking my coffee.' He placed his hands on either side of her on the bed and deliberately caged her in. She smelt of lilies, her amazing eyes had his heart stuttering and it took every bit of willpower he had not to lower his mouth to hers.

'So, you have two choices. You get your very pretty butt out of bed, into some old clothes—or, in your case, clothes that you don't mind getting dirty—and get into my vehicle in—' he looked at his watch '—thirteen minutes or you work in your pyjamas. If you don't want to work, then ask Daddy to send his jet for you but, until it arrives, you will work. Are we clear?'

Clem held the cup near her mouth and he could see that her fingers were trembling. She held his gaze for a minute and he saw the realization dawn that he was as serious as a snake bite.

'But what am I going to do? I don't work! I've never worked!' she wailed.

'Then it's high time you started,' Nick suggested and told himself to stand up. He had to repeat the instruction because he was fascinated by the collection of tiny freckles on her nose. 'Twelve minutes, Red.'

When he reached the door he heard her sigh and the rustle of bedclothes. 'You are the most high-handed, arrogant, annoying man I've ever met.'

Nick grinned. 'Well, your opinion of me is sure to deteriorate as the day marches on.'

In fact, he could practically guarantee it.

She made it to the vehicle with thirty seconds to spare and clambered over the passenger door, not bothering to try opening the door. Ha, he hadn't thought she could get ready in time...points for me, Clem thought as she sat down, trying to avoid the broken spring.

'What are you wearing?' he demanded.

Clem looked down at her vintage studded denim shorts, frayed at the hem. Admittedly, she usually wore these to go clubbing in, but they also worked with the lace vest she'd pulled on.

'A taffeta ball gown, obviously.'

'Those shorts would be declared illegal in some countries. If you were wearing anything shorter, it would be a thong.'

'Rubbish.'

Clem sat back and mused that she would rather eat worms than admit to Nick that she was glad to be out of the house, that his guest room was becoming claustrophobic and that she could see herself going slowly out of her mind with boredom if she stayed in there one more day.

Even his stupid Lodge and stupider vehicle and this back of beyond place were a welcome relief from the white walls and her own company. She was pretty good at sulking, even better at wallowing, but a girl could only keep it up for a finite length of time.

Yeah, she'd rather eat worms and *slugs* than admit that.

Clem turned in her seat. 'So, what do you want me to do? I'm good at talking to people, so I could work with your guests.'

'I wouldn't let you anywhere near my guests,' Nick said, picking up a coffee cup from between his knees and raising it to his lips. Clem sighed; she hadn't had a chance to have any more of her coffee than a couple of quick hot gulps.

'So, because I'm basically a reasonable guy, you get a choice of duties.'

Yeah, reasonable like the Black Friday or January sales shoppers.

'The Baobab and Buffalo Lodge and Animal Rehabilitation Centre employs trainee game rangers and they start at the bottom of the food chain. In addition to their studies—fauna and flora—they are the general skivvies.' Nick smiled. 'You're the latest intern.'

'So, do people do this willingly or do you blackmail them into being slaves for you too?' Clem demanded.

'Blackmail is a harsh word but, in your case, remarkably accurate.' Nick rested his elbow on the steering wheel. The morning sun caught his two day stubble and picked up the sun-lightened tips of his hair. He looked tough and hard in his Two-B uniform of a navy-blue golf shirt and khaki shorts, a tiny tree embroidered onto the pocket of his shirt above the company name.

This morning his eyes were the shade of moonlight.

'Normally, I'd never give interns a choice of duties but what the hell. You can clean out the staff bar, called The Pit for a reason. On good nights you need a tetanus jab to go in.'

Clem pretended to think. 'No.'

'Ironing? Sheets, duvets, pillowcases.'

'Still no.'

'Cleaning toilets?'

'As if.'

She couldn't do this, Clem thought. Maybe she should just bite the bullet and go back to London. How bad could it be…? She'd be stalked and hassled by the press everywhere she went but they'd back off. Eventually.

On the plus side, there would be no cleaning, ironing and skanky bars to clean.

Clem stared at her hands and opened her mouth to tell Nick to call her father and ask him for the jet. He beat her to the punch.

'Yeah, I thought so. You're just good at looking decorative.'

Clem stared at him as his dismissive words sliced deeper and deeper until they hit her soul.

Temper, hot and wild, shot up from the core of her being and flashed in her eyes. 'What did you say to me?' she hissed.

'I—'

'How dare you? You don't get to say that to me. Nobody says that to me any more.'

'Red…'

'I took it from him for far too many years but I will not

take it from you!' Clem shouted. Her hands gripped the edge of the ragged seat as she started to shake. Her voice was wobbly but her words were coated with determination. 'I can take anything that you throw at me.'

Clem, feeling as if she was having an out of body experience, looked at her furious other self and shook her head. No, she couldn't. She was a pampered society girl...

'You sure about that, Princess?'

No, not at all sure. Clem wanted to recant but the crazy woman inside had her biting her tongue instead. 'Do your worst.'

She looked at Nick's handsome, amused face and his certainty that she would fail stiffened her spine. How dare he dismiss her, assume that he knew her? She was *not* just a pretty face. She *did* have more depth than the average puddle.

Maybe. Hopefully.

'I won't quit,' she muttered, mostly to herself.

The man had ears like a bat. 'Oh, you so will,' Nick assured her.

She gritted her teeth. 'Watch me. Do your damnedest, Sherwood.'

'Seriously?' Nick laughed. 'Are you challenging me?'

'Yeah. I'm tired of stupid men telling me what I am and am not, what I can and cannot do.' Clem caught the speculative look in his eye and wondered if she hadn't pushed him a touch too far.

Two voices were clamouring for air time in her head.

Just call your father and go home, the coward in her begged.

But the louder voice was more encouraging. *You can do anything you want to. You're only good at looking decorative, my sweet butt.*

That voice sounded strong and powerful and sounded as if it knew what it was talking about.

CHAPTER THREE

Luella Dawson's blog:

So, we had a taster of the second series of The Crazy Cs from the interview I did with Cai and his new lady-love. They were in his home in LA, into which Kiki has been installed. One word, Cai—tacky! Then again, the man is taking tacky to a new art form lately.

So, was anyone more bored than me? I've had more fun watching mould form. Kiki is vapid and moronic and, as for that rat-on-a-rope she calls a dog? Pathetic! Come back, Clem! All is forgiven!

NICK drove into the staff village, past a building that had 'The Pit' stencilled across it and past the fenced off swimming pool. Veering left, away from the amenities and the houses, he made for an isolated corner, just inside the electric fence and hidden from view by a split-pole fence. He pulled the Land Rover up, hopped out and stood at the entrance.

The smell of decomposing garbage had Clem wrinkling her nose. 'What are we doing here?'

'This is our recycling centre.' He led her into the enclosure, where black refuse bags were piled up on the hard packed dirt. He pulled a pair of heavy gloves off the fence and handed them to her.

Four large skips were lined up against the fence. 'Glass, paper, tin and plastic.' He nudged a black bag. 'What's in here goes in there.' He pointed to the skips. 'Glass in glass, paper in paper...organic matter goes on the compost heap over there. The staff are supposed to recycle but it doesn't always happen.'

Clem, her heart sinking to her toes, shook her head. 'Oh, no, this is too cruel. I'm wearing designer espadrilles.'

'Hey, you said to throw my worst at you. This is it.'

Of course it was. Clem bit her lip. 'So, I presume you're leaving me alone here?'

'Yep.' Nick pulled a spare radio from his back pocket and handed it to her. 'You're within the electric fence so you're good, animal wise. The radio is already set on the open channel, number two, press this button to talk. Anything you say on this channel will be broadcast to every staff member who has a radio. If you want to talk to me in private, call me and ask me to switch to channel thirteen.'

Clem took the radio and kicked the sand with her shoe, trying not to breathe. She tucked the radio into the band between her shorts and stomach and looked around, trying not to cry. 'So, you'll pick me up in about eight hours?'

Nick laughed, shook his head and tapped her nose. 'No, Red, not even I am that cruel. Stick it out for the morning and we'll call it a draw.' He sent her a speculative look. 'But that actually means you have to do some work, not just sitting on your butt. If you don't work, you will do a double shift tomorrow.'

So he wasn't a fool... She'd been planning on finding the least smelly area and waiting him out. A morning, Clem thought. She could do this for a morning. She put her hands on her hips and watched Nick walk away, then drive off. She desperately wanted to run after him but stubborn pride kept her feet glued to the spot. Then she sat down in the sand and looked around.

Crap. Figuratively.

And, obviously, literally.

7.05 a.m.

Clem, knee deep in rubbish, lifted her hot heavy hair off her neck and yanked the perspiration-covered radio from her shorts. She couldn't do this, she really couldn't. She wanted to go home…she wanted a macchiato, a hot stone massage, sushi. She wanted her life back, damn it!

She pushed the call button to cry uncle. 'Nick, this is Clem.'

'Giving up already, Red?'

I was until you said that. 'No, I thought I'd just let you know that I think you are a loathsome toad.'

'Switch to channel thirteen, Red, if you're going to curse me.'

'Oh, I haven't even started to curse you and I think I'll stay on the open channel. People of Two-B, your boss is a loathsome toad.'

'You said that already.'

'Give me a minute to come up with something a bit more creative.'

9.35 a.m.

Nick, sitting down at a table in the staff dining room, remembered that Clem hadn't eaten yet. He sighed, thumbed his radio and called in. 'You hungry, Red?'

Clem's voice was sharper than the canine teeth on a leopard. 'I'm knee-deep in fetid organic waste, gunky tin cans and soaked paper, Sherwood. Of course I'm not hungry. *Tu es complètement débile!*'

Nick looked up, saw the amusement on the faces of his staff and raised a hand. 'I know I'm going to regret this, but can anyone translate?'

Janet, a junior receptionist, giggled. 'Um, I think she called you a moron, boss.'

Nick hauled in a deep breath. Giving her a radio was not his brightest idea. 'Channel thirteen, Red.'

'Bite me.'

10.45 a.m.

'Nick…'

Was he ever going to get any work done today? 'What now?'

'There's a monkey.'

Nick stared at the requisition form in front of him and dashed his signature at the bottom of the page. 'Uh huh. We have them. What's it doing?'

'Looking at me.'

'Looking at you how?'

'Um…just looking. Kind of cocking its head…'

Nick grinned. 'Maybe it's just surprised to see an It girl in a rubbish dump. Ignore the monkey and get back to work, Princess.'

Nick picked her up at twelve and Clem ran out to meet the Landy, barely allowing him to stop before hopping up on the running board.

'It's about time you got here.'

Nick put his hand to his nose when she climbed up next to him. Shaking his head, he jerked his thumb to the back seat. 'There is no way you're sitting next to me!'

'Why not?'

'Because you reek? Good grief, what did you do? Roll in something dead? Sit in the back, on the edge of the back seat and as far away from me as possible.'

Clem considered refusing, then the thought occurred to her that he might make her walk home, wild animals or not. She was tired and stiff and…starving. So she climbed over to the back seat, sat on the edge and held onto it with a death grip. If she fell out and he drove over her then it would serve him right! Not that that would work for her…but she'd like to see him trying to explain her demise to her father.

Hah…whoah! She wobbled and clutched the seat in front of her. 'Will you take it easy? I'm used to sitting on a seat!'

On the drive back to the house, Clem's eyes kept returning to the back of his strong neck, the breadth of his shoulders. He needed a haircut and she spent far too much time looking at his hands, easy on the wheel. They were worker's hands, she thought. Tanned, with short nails, a couple of nicks and scars. He held the wheel like she'd imagine he'd hold a woman, easily and competently, as if he'd been doing it his whole life.

She wondered how they would feel on her skin…

'Red, we're here.'

Nick's voice shattered her reverie and she jerked her eyes up and looked around. They were parked on the patch of grass outside his house so she stood up and jumped down from the side of the Landy, her ruined shoes in her fingers. She looked at them and sighed… Poor shoes.

Clem started for the house but a pair of fingers snagged the waistband of her denim shorts and she was brought to a sudden halt.

'What—?'

'Where do you think you are going?' Nick growled.

'I am going to shower.'

'You are not going into my house smelling like that,' Nick told her, pulling her backwards. Clem twisted in an effort to get out his grip and nearly managed it until a strong arm bounded around her waist and hauled her against his chest.

Nick swore. 'You've given me your stench! Damn it, Red!'

He easily held her with one hand and grabbed hold of the spigot of the garden hose, flipping the tap open with his knee. Without warning, he dropped Clem and turned the hose on her and she gasped when a stream of cold water hit her in the face.

Clem slapped her hands to her face and turned her back to the deluge. '*Nick*!'

'Princess?' The water hit her shoulder, the back of her neck, drenched her hair.

'I'm going to disembowel and string you up for the hyenas!' she shouted in between her splutters.

'You can try,' Nick said, aiming the water at her bottom. 'What on earth did you sit in, Red?'

Clem twisted to look. 'A bag burst and I slipped. I think it's a mixture of rotten tomatoes and cabbage.' She tipped her head back as Nick aimed the water at her chest. 'Actually, that's kind of nice. It's the first time I've felt cool since I got here.'

'I think that's a spinach leaf on your ankle.'

'Eeew.' Clem reached down and picked the leaf off her skin. 'So, am I clean enough to go into your precious house?'

'Not in those clothes. Strip.'

Clem lifted her eyebrows. 'I beg your pardon?'

Nick looked impatient. And amused. 'I can still smell you and ninety per cent of the smell is in your clothes. I'll get you a towel if you're feeling modest.'

Oh, she was very tired of that smirky smile, that expression that said he was dealing with the village idiot. He wanted her to strip?

Well, OK then...

Clem narrowed her eyes and, without removing her annoyed gaze from his face, lifted her vest and pulled it up and over her head and dropped it to the grass. Standing in her low-cut lacy scarlet bra, she reached for the snap of her denims.

Nick tried to looked insouciant but she saw the telltale muscle jump in his jaw. So she flipped open the buttons and deliberately wiggled her shorts down her legs, slowly revealing a brief pair of matching panties. The hosepipe in Nick's hand dropped as she stepped out of the denims—destined to be burnt—and she swung her hips as she sauntered up to him.

His eyes were everywhere they shouldn't be and, for once, she was OK with that because he didn't notice what she was doing. In a flash she lifted the pipe and directed a stream of water at his crotch before whipping it up and directing it into his open-with-shock mouth.

Grinning, she dropped the hose and, listening to him splutter, walked into the house. She hadn't been a lingerie model for nothing.

When Nick brought Clem back to the house it was after five and she was shattered. She showered, hopped out and could still smell the rubbish dump on her skin so she hopped back in. She'd used up half a bottle of her favourite shampoo and she still reeked of…something vile.

It had been a dismal day, she decided. After her hose down—with neither of them referring to her impromptu striptease—a shower and a huge salad sandwich in the staff canteen at lunch time, Nick had carted her off to the laundry room, where she was given a pile of sheets to iron. After she'd burnt two million-thread count Egyptian cotton sheets, the housekeeper had thrown a hissy fit, picked up the sheet and cursed her in her native language. She'd been hustled out of the laundry, told that she was useless, that she was making the sheets smell and was put to work cleaning out The Pit.

That was an experience she'd rather not repeat. Not as bad as the recycling but sticky floors, grimy bar, dirty glasses. Ugh.

Clem pulled on a sleeveless sage-green patterned top, cream shorts and flip-flops and walked into the lounge, towelling her hair dry.

Nick was also freshly showered, dressed in white cargo shorts and a button down navy shirt, and he looked up from his laptop that sat on the kitchen counter.

'Do you want a glass of wine? Or a beer?'

'Something soft?' Clem responded, rubbing the ends of her hair. 'I don't drink alcohol.'

Nick looked surprised. 'At all?'

'Yeah. And no, I'm not a recovering alcoholic, nor have any addiction problems. My mum was killed in a car accident and the other driver was drunk and stoned.'

Why had she told him that? Apart from the very rare comment to Jason, she never discussed her mother with anyone.

'I'm sorry.' Nick turned away from her and looked in the fridge. He pulled out a box of fruit juice. 'This OK?'

'Thanks.' Clem watched him as he pulled out a glass and poured her juice. Their fingers brushed as he handed the glass over and sparks shot up her arm. OK, now she was just being pathetic.

Clem bunched the towel in her hand and wrinkled her nose. 'Nick, I still stink.'

Nick grinned and her heart pitter-pattered. 'I'm sure you don't.'

Clem shook her head, and lifted her forearm to her nose. 'I can still smell it. Can you?'

Nick put his beer down and walked over to her, his feet bare on the wooden floor. Standing beside her, her heartbeat picked up when he took her arm and lifted her wrist to his nose. He shook his head and Clem sucked in her breath as he sniffed his way up her arm, past her elbow and onto her shoulder. Clem stood statue-still, trying not to squirm as his nose tickled the wet hair under her ear. He lifted her heavy hair with his hand, wrapped it around his fist and moved his nose across the back on her neck, her shoulder and down her other arm.

By that time, all the saliva in her mouth had disappeared and her limbs were heavy with desire.

Oh no, this wasn't good.

Nick dropped her hair and stepped away from her. When

she felt some of her self-control returning, she looked at him. He'd moved to the other side of the kitchen counter and was scowling at his laptop screen.

'I think it's your hair,' Nick eventually said, his voice low.

Her hair? What about her hair…? Oh, the stink. Get a grip, Clem.

She had stinky hair. Ick. Well, she could sort that out. And easily. Clem slung the towel over her shoulder and moved to the kitchen. 'Do you have a pair of scissors?'

Nick looked up and she noticed that his eyes had changed from moonlight to the colour of dark thunder clouds. Heavy, passionate. If she didn't know better, she'd think that he looked as turned-on as she was. That was ridiculous on so many levels that it simply wasn't possible.

'Uh, somewhere.' Nick shoved his hand into his wet hair and sent her a bemused look. 'Study desk, top drawer. Maybe.'

'Thanks.'

Clem either underestimated the thickness of her hair or over-estimated the sharpness of the scissors. Or both. She'd pulled her hair back, tied it at the neck and held it tightly in the circle of her thumb and index finger. The scissors cut the outside layer of her hair and then gave up the ghost.

Damn it; she'd started the process and she couldn't stop now.

'Nick?' she called from her bathroom.

'Yeah?'

'Can you come and help me for a minute? Would you mind?'

A minute later, Nick appeared in the doorway to her bath-room. 'What the hell are you doing, Red?' His eyes widened when he saw the scissors in her hand. 'Oh, Clem, no.'

She shrugged. 'It's just hair. My hair is either too thick for the scissors or the scissors are blunt, but it's not working.'

'Well, leave it! Why would you do this?' Nick sounded almost panicked.

Clem kept a tight hold of her hair. 'I can't leave it. I've started already. Can you try and cut the rest off?'

Nick shook his head and took the scissors from her hand, running his thumb along the blade. 'Blunt as hell. Wait here, you crazy person.'

Nick was back in under a minute, a sharp, lethal hunting knife in his hand. Clem lifted an eyebrow. 'Are you planning on doing me in at the same time?'

Nick stepped into the bathroom and stood behind her with both of them facing the mirror. 'Considering it. You should be shot at dawn for hacking off your hair.' His eyes met her miserable ones in the mirror. 'Why?'

Clem lifted her shoulder. 'It stinks and it was so hot today and...'

'You could've pinned it up and the stink isn't that bad. Tell me the truth, Clem,' Nick said as he nudged her hand away to hold her hair in a tight grip.

'I've wanted to cut it for ever. About six years ago, I cut about six inches off and Cai went nuts. I thought he was going to kill me.'

Behind her, Clem felt Nick stiffen. 'He hurt you?'

'No. He wanted to but he knew that was a step too far. He did threaten me, though, said that if I ever cut it, I'd regret it. I guess he frightened me enough that I was too scared to try.' Clem looked into his hard, angry face. 'I'm not scared any more and if I want to cut my hair, I will.'

'Was he the one who told you that your sole value was in your looks?'

Clem bit her lip. 'You caught that then?'

'Pretty big trigger. You did a one-eighty in two seconds flat.' Nick looked at the back of her head and winced. 'I can't believe I'm about to do this. OK, hold still. I don't want you jerking and the knife slipping. It's seriously sharp.'

Clem grinned. 'Yeah, explaining my death to my father might not be easy.' She saw his hesitation and reached back to pat his thigh. 'It's OK, Nick. Just do it.'

The knife slid under her hair, slipped through like butter and within seconds Nick stood with a hunk of hair in his hand. Clem laughed and ran her hands through her hair, swinging her head. 'Yay! Oh, that feels so good.'

'It's a little uneven at the back. Maybe one of the girls in the spa can cut it straight,' Nick suggested.

'I don't care!' Clem did a little twirl. 'Oh, I look so different. I love it, love it!'

Nick held up the hair in his hand. 'What do you want to do with this?'

'Oh, toss it! Um…maybe not. I'll keep it and donate it to one of those organizations that make wigs for cancer patients. I'm sure they could use it.' Clem took her hair and sniffed it. 'Or maybe not. Eeew.'

Nick smiled as he slid his knife back into its sheath. 'Put it in the sun to air. The smell will go, eventually.' He backed out of the bathroom and stopped at the door. 'You look good, Red.'

Clem looked at herself in the mirror and had to agree. She did look good. Her hair, drying quickly, had jumped back into its natural curls and fell into a natural tousled bob. It was the best haircut she'd ever had and it had taken two seconds flat with a hunting knife.

Clem looked at her face and her dancing eyes and suddenly thought, *Oh wow, so that's what I look like when I smile. I almost didn't recognize myself.*

He had to get rid of her, Nick decided, as he walked back into the lounge, rubbing the back of his neck as he did so. She was wild and crazy—what the hell was she thinking cutting off her stunning hair on a whim?—but he wanted her.

Since the moment he'd seen her stepping off that plane

he'd imagined those long, slim, pale legs wrapping around his hips, her head on his pillow, those come-to-bed eyes staring up into his. It had taken every last vestige of his self-control to stop himself from banding his arms around her waist and kissing every inch of that smooth skin he'd earlier sniffed.

He was attracted to her because she was a stunning woman and he was a man who hadn't had any for a while.

Except that now and then, when he forgot that she was a spoilt city brat who needed her attitude adjusted, he caught a glimpse of someone, somewhere who intrigued him. He suspected that she, like her father, had a wicked sense of humour and, more frightening, unplumbed depths. He sure as hell hadn't expected her to last more than an hour at the dump but, unlike some of his previous employees, she hadn't given up, hadn't thrown in the towel.

He had to respect that...

She had to leave and soon, before he did something stupid, like throw her over his shoulder and take her to bed.

Because, apart from the fact that they were oil and water, city and country, she was coming out of a complicated long-term relationship. Ten years together wasn't married but damn close.

Getting involved with her, on any level, would be the equivalent of a dumpster fire: awkward, chaotic and, eventually, just plain ugly.

He had very few rules for his life but avoiding complicated situations was one of them. Followed closely by not taking emotionally side-winded, rejected, possibly crazy, definitely intriguing women to bed.

Why didn't he just get it over with and actually shoot himself in the foot? It would be easier and far less painful in the long run.

Nick stepped out onto the deck and sank into one of the loungers, resting his aching head—he wished that was the only part of his body that was aching—on the cushion he tucked behind his head. Waterbuck, giraffe, kudu and Egyptian geese were at the waterhole.

Clem stepped onto the deck, her glass of juice in her hand. She looked different without her swathe of hair—stronger, freer and lighter.

'Oh, this is great.' Clem immediately echoed his favourite stance, forearms on the railing, bum in the air. The fabric of her shorts pulled and defined her butt and Nick coughed, sprang up and joined her at the railing, willing his body to behave.

'I recognize the giraffe but not much more,' Clem said.

'You will,' Nick assured her. 'There's a pile of books on the dining room table. Your study material.'

'What?'

'All the interns have to study while they are here, in addition to their normal duties. Land management, conservation, identification of animals, birds and flora.' Nick pointed out a herd of buffalo that were ambling down to the waterhole. 'And there's my girl.'

'What? Where?'

Nick pointed to a thicket north-east of the pan. 'A rhino cow. She tends to hang around this area.' Nick smiled at the prehistoric beast. 'Hello, gorgeous. How are you doing? We're going to bring you some friends soon.'

Clem arched her spectacular brows. 'Do you often talk to animals?'

'All the time.'

'And do the rhinos have play dates?'

Nick looked down into her dancing eyes and realized that she was joking. His mouth kicked up. 'I bought some rhinos from another reserve and am trying to raise the cash to pay for their translocation. It's seriously expensive and I don't have it right now.'

'Ask my father for it.'

Nick snorted. 'Is that your answer for everything,

Princess?' He didn't bother to wait for her reply. 'I'll find the cash, somewhere. I just hope they can hold on.'

'Are they that desperate for company?'

She *really* didn't know anything about wildlife. 'No, you twit, they are solitary animals. Rhinos are highly endangered and the incidents of poaching have gone through the roof. I need to move the crash I bought from a reserve in the north to Two-B.'

Clem drained her juice and fluffed her hair. Nick smiled; she seemed to be liking her short hair. He did too. They watched the waterhole in silence until Clem spoke.

'Does the Lodge overlook this waterhole?'

'Not this one; a bigger one,' Nick replied.

Clem's eyes clashed with his and he immediately noticed that they were darker, hotter, that the pulse point in her throat was pumping. She swallowed, straightened and licked her lips. No, don't do that, he silently told her.

His bed wasn't that far away.

Dumpster fire...

Nick thought it was high time he brought them both back down to earth. 'So, a couple of house rules.'

Clem winced. 'More rules?'

'I don't have a daily maid service so you make your own bed, tidy up after yourself, toss the dishes in the dishwasher, your clothes in the washing machine,' he told her and watched her eyes widen. 'Twice a week, either Mama Thembi or Mama Sophie will be driven down and they'll mop and dust and change the linens. That reminds me, you owe me four hundred pounds for the two sheets you destroyed.'

'Put it on my bill. I think your housekeeper put a curse on me, she yelled at me so loudly.'

'I wouldn't be surprised.' Nick succumbed to the urge to touch her and placed his hand on her neck, easily encircling most of her neck with his fingers. He pushed her towards the sliding door and into the lounge. 'Let's eat dinner in the staff dining room.'

Clem sent him a mischievous look. 'Not at the Lodge?'

'Keep dreaming, Red.'

'When do I get to see your precious Lodge, by the way?'

Nick glanced at his watch. 'Now, if you want. I need to stop by my office and most of the guests will be out on the evening game drive.'

'Great.' Clem followed him out of the house and towards his vehicle. She climbed into his Landy and stared down at the seat. 'Are you ever going to fix this seat?'

'Maybe. When you stop being a pain.'

CHAPTER FOUR

Luella Dawson's blog:

> *You'll never guess where she is! Our Clem, city girl and glamour babe girlfriend, is on a game reserve in the deepest Africa and no, folks, it's not April Fools day! I was told by my very reliable source that she's staying with a very hot, very single, very sexy lodge owner. Fireworks are guaranteed!*
>
> *Will keep you posted as I get tweets in my ear!*

AFTER following Nick through the exquisitely decorated Lodge—library, business centre, a cigar bar, three different dining rooms, three public lounges—Clem found herself seriously impressed. It was tasteful, clever and, above all, very, very rich.

Nick gestured her to walk out onto the covered veranda that ran the length of the house and provided superb views of the jackelberry and acacia thorn tree bush and the watering hole at the bottom of the cliff. Below the veranda the landscaper had created a series of rock lined terraces filled with emerald green grass. The last of the terraces contained a sparkling lap pool edged with a wooden deck. The guests could hang on the opposite side of the pool and feel as if they were on the edge of the world, about to be swept into the landscape below, Clem thought.

'We also have the private villa and the tented camp deeper into the reserve,' Nick told her, putting his hands into the pockets of his cargo shorts.

Clem returned the greeting of a butler who walked up to them. Nick refused his offer for a drink and Clem reminded him to tell her about the private villa. 'Six en-suite bedrooms with en suite bathrooms; I built it to cater for extended families or groups of friends. It has a heated swimming pool and a huge deck overlooking another waterhole often visited by the Big Five.' Nick nodded to another butler and continued, 'Guests have a private game-viewing vehicle and a ranger, personal chef and masseuse at their disposal.'

'Serious luxury, serious money.'

'Oh yeah. Now, the tented camp is very different. Luxurious, yes, but a lot more rugged. No electricity, canvas showers, no electric fence. Very, very isolated, very quiet.'

Clem looked around and whistled. 'It's a hell of a place, Nick.'

'I couldn't have done it if your father hadn't provided the capital. I owe him.'

'And that's why I landed on your doorstep.'

'Yeah.' Nick turned at footsteps behind them and grinned at a tall blonde, dressed in a khaki skirt and a Two-B blue golf shirt. 'Hey, Megan. Megs, Clem Copeland. Megan is my Lodge manager.'

Megan didn't even blink when Nick introduced her. She'd probably had so many celebrities through the Lodge that it was now old hat to her. It was nice, Clem thought. Different but nice.

'Nick. Hi, Clem.' Megan glanced down at the slip she held in her hand and looked back at Clem. 'I'm glad I caught you both; I was just about to radio you. A Jason Feinstein has been trying to reach you, Clem. He says it's important and he's waiting for you to Skype him.'

Clem frowned. 'He wouldn't be calling unless something else has gone wrong. Can I call him?'

'We'll take it in my office. Thanks, Megs.'

Clem followed Nick but stopped when Megan called her name.

'I'd never normally do this but I'd just like to tell you that I'm sorry. He was truly awful.'

Clem blinked and dipped her head. 'Thank you. So has everyone in the Lodge seen the interview?'

She grimaced. 'Pretty much.'

Clem tried to shrug it off. 'Well, I'm pretty sure there are tribes in the Amazon who haven't seen it.'

'I haven't,' Nick said as she reached him. He nudged her through a door marked 'Private—Staff only'.

'Why not?' Clem asked him, curious.

'Hey, I have to live with you, I don't need to see or hear any more of you than I already do.'

Fair enough, Clem thought.

Clem stared at Jason on the computer screen in horror. This could not be happening. She risked a look at Nick, whose face was equally thunderous.

'There is no question, it's not happening.' She repeated her internal statement in a wobbly voice.

Nick leaned over her shoulder and stared at the screen. 'Let me get this straight. Some production company wants to film Clem as she deals with her breakup from Campbell?'

'Essentially.'

'That's sick,' Nick stated.

'That's showbiz.' Jason shrugged. 'The thing is that the production company have the option to extend the contract for another ten episodes if they so want to, and they do.'

Nick turned to Clem, his face perplexed. 'You agreed to this?'

Clem shrugged. 'Cai agreed to it. I just went along for the ride.'

'That's a terrible excuse,' Nick snapped.

'And you did sign the contract agreeing to them filming the extra episodes,' Jason stated, looking miserable. 'How many times did I tell you not to sign stuff Cai handed to you?'

Nick stood up and shook his head, obviously disgusted by her stupidity. But he didn't realise that, with Cai, it was frequently just easier to go with the flow than fight the tsunami.

Clem rested her chin on her fist. 'So where do I go from here?'

Jason looked as if he'd swallowed a poisonous bug. 'Well, I checked with your lawyers and the bottom line is that if you don't do it they can sue you sideways.'

'For what?' Clem cried.

'Loss of income, not honouring the terms of the contract, blah blah. It's two weeks of filming, Clemmie, they recommend that you just do it.'

'When hell freezes over,' Clem muttered but she knew he was right. It was also a good excuse to leave this place... But she wasn't sure she wanted to.

And where did that thought come from? Just this morning she had been desperate to leave. And where did this need to prove to Nick that she was more than a fluffy airhead come from? *And why did she care?*

'I have a suggestion...' Clem looked at the screen and saw Jason take a deep breath. She recognized that look and knew that whatever was coming would be far left of centre.

'What?'

'I think you should film at Nick's Lodge.'

'I think you should get your head examined,' Nick growled.

Jason ignored him. 'Clem, it would be a great way to "rehabilitate" your reputation.'

'Excuse me? Is my rep that bad?'

'Yes, in a way. Although the world sympathizes with what Cai did to you, the sympathy doesn't run that deep. You're a young, rich, beautiful woman who wafts around doing nothing and some people think that you deserved what you got.'

'That's harsh.'

'That's reality. If they could see you doing something worthwhile, working at something, somewhere so out of your depth for a good cause—don't you run an animal rehabilitation centre, Nick?—they would lap it up.' Jason looked smug and Clem thought he had a right to be. It would be great PR.

Clem sucked in her bottom lip and looked at Nick. 'What do you think?'

'No, no and hell, no!'

Jason spoke again. 'Nick, it would be a win win situation. Millions watched the last season and the exposure for your foundation would be enormous. Donations would flood in.'

Nick folded his arms and looked formidable. 'I can't have people filming my Lodge, the guests. I don't want people filming me.'

Jason chimed in. 'That would be one of the provisos. No filming of the lodge or guests. You'd have to be filmed, and your staff, but no guests.'

'They get what they need for ten episodes in two weeks and that's it, nothing more. Two cameras, run and gun. I get to call a halt on anything I'm not comfortable with. So does Nick,' Clem stated.

'No problem.' Jason nodded and jotted some notes on the pad in front of him.

'I'm not saying yes to this,' Nick stated. 'It's not going to happen.'

Clem stood up and looked him in the eye. 'Yes, it is. You've already considered it a couple of times because your foundation needs that money and fast. So, I'll sweeten the pot. I'll match any donation you get via the show, capped at five hundred thousand dollars. That's my fee for doing this additional series.'

Nick blinked. 'What?'

'They pay me to do this series, Nick.' She turned to Jason. 'They do pay me, don't they?'

'Of course they do.'

'So, I'll pay you, Nick. I'll give you a down payment of fifty thousand dollars, right now, non-refundable.'

'You're going to pay me fifty grand to do this?'

'Yes, and I'll match every donation to five hundred grand. For that, you give me a few weeks of your time.' Clem angled her head, hoping he couldn't see her heart jumping out of her chest. Say yes, Nick. I don't want to leave yet...

'Think of those rhinos, Nick.'

'You play dirty, Copeland,' Nick sighed and Clem knew she'd won. She just stopped herself from punching the air.

Clem nodded to Jason, who said a quick goodbye and disappeared. Nick stepped closer to Clem and sent her an enigmatic look. 'If we are going to have cameras in our faces for the next two weeks, then there's something I've got to do first.'

'What?'

'This.'

Nick stepped forward, gripped her wrist and yanked her against his chest. His mouth slanted over hers and she thought that he was more than she'd imagined—darker, spicier, hotter. When her mouth opened he plummeted inside...and the air around them exploded. Power clashed with power, need with need. Tongues darted and teeth scraped and the world spun off its axis as his arms banded around her as they feasted.

It had been so long since she'd been touched—touched properly—and she'd missed it, missed...this. Missed feeling so completely at ease—physically—in a man's arms, missed knowing that someone knew exactly what she liked, and needed.

She'd never had him but she'd missed him. It made no sense.

It was Nick who lifted his head on a groan, Nick who pulled away. He looked down at her with eyes that were miserable and passionate, determined but longing. 'Damn it.'

Clem made a sound between a snort and a laugh. 'It's been a long time since I've kissed anyone beside that loser but I'm pretty sure that's not a good response.'

Nick picked up her left hand and grabbed her ring finger, where a square centimetre pink diamond glinted. 'You're coming out of a long-term relationship. I don't do emotionally battered women.'

'I haven't been in a real relationship for a long time,' Clem said quietly. 'Not in a way that meant anything.'

'Yeah, well, I don't believe that and I have no intention of being your stepping stone back to normality. That was the first and last time that'll happen.'

Clem looked at him from under her lashes. 'Why don't we make that the second and last time?'

Nick held out for about ten seconds before he dived in, cradling her head in his hands, turning her head to deepen the kiss. Then one of his hands slid down her back to her bottom, the other was spread between her shoulder blades, both pushing her so that her breasts pressed against his chest and his thigh pushed between her legs.

Clem whimpered in his mouth, utterly at the mercy of the hands, his mouth. Unable to stop herself, she slid her hands up and under his shirt, across the long muscles in his back, round to his stomach and the six-pack she knew was lurking under his clothing. Her fingers tap danced their way across the ridges and it felt so natural to let them drift lower...

Nick sprang back and away from her as he muttered an obscenity. Clem staggered back, her hands looking for the desk she thought was somewhere behind her. She felt the smooth wood and clutched the edge, hoping that her knees would lock some time in the near future.

Clem clutched at any straw she could find. 'I kissed you because I'm on the rebound,' she gabbled. 'I haven't had sex for the best part of a year and, honestly, I haven't had good sex in, well, forever.'

And I'm attracted to him because he's the exact opposite of Cai—reticent, reserved, quietly commanding, introspective and, damn it, mostly calm, Clem thought. Not when he kissed her, obviously, but generally.

She bit her lip and kept her eyes on her feet. 'So why did you kiss me?'

'Because I'm an idiot,' Nick retorted. 'I'll see you at the car.'

Clem blew out her cheeks 'Again, not quite the response I was looking for.'

Later in the week, Clem, tired of being on the receiving end of Nick's drill sergeant style of getting her out of bed every morning, decided it was high time that she gave him a dose of his own medicine. They had an even earlier start this morning because they had to fly to the town of Mbom-something to pick up the film crew for the show, so Clem knew she had to get up ultra-early to give Nick a taste of what his yelling at her put her through every morning.

So she set her alarm for forty-five minutes earlier and eventually got up when it blared at her for the third time. Or was it fourth? Anyway, the lengths she would go to for revenge...

She dressed in a pair of beige hipster shorts and a white tank top that rode up her stomach and slid her feet into a pair of funky beaded flip-flops. With her teeth and hair brushed, eyelashes mascara-ed, she quietly made coffee and, seeing she had time, perched on the dining table to enjoy the relative quiet of the early morning.

Clem looked across the lounge and deck and sighed at the band of mist that hovered over the waterhole and swirled around the trunks of the trees. What was she doing here? With Cai, she'd lived the life of a pampered poodle—emotionally kicked around admittedly—but with every comfort and amenity available to her. She hadn't lifted a finger, made a bed or washed a dish in over a decade.

Yet she'd been restless, unfulfilled and unhappy.

Here, at Two-B, she had her nose to the grindstone ten hours a day, ate good but not gourmet meals and was up at the crack of dawn daily.

And she felt... How did she feel? Tired, obviously, and frequently at sea because she didn't know what she was doing half the time, and irritated because Nick was so *bossy...*

But she wasn't bored and she wasn't unhappy. She wasn't happy, precisely, but she did feel...oh, damn it, how could she admit this? Secure. For the first time in her life, she felt secure enough to be herself...whoever that might be.

She was still trying to work that out. But finding out who she was and not who anybody else expected her to be was... Clem searched for the word to describe the emotion she felt bubbling inside. Frightening? Yes. Exciting? Hell, yes. Liberating? So, so liberating.

Clem smiled at herself and rolled her head. She was stiff again. Tipping her head to stretch out her muscles, her eyes fell on a piece a paper on the table next to her thigh.

Although peppered with figures, Clem could see that it was originally a document stating the rates for the Lodge, private villa and tented camp. She whistled soundlessly. Even she, no stranger to whipping out her credit card and flinging it about, raised her eyebrows at the prices he charged.

Nicholas, Nicholas... What was she going to do about him? Since their hot and steamy encounter at the Lodge, they'd been even ruder to each other than normal in an effort to pretend that kiss hadn't happened.

But it had and it did and she couldn't stop thinking about it. She'd tossed and turned every night since, reliving the feel of his lips, the texture of his skin under her fingertips, the heat and hardness of that spectacular body...

Checking her watch, she smiled, picked up the other—now lukewarm—cup of coffee and quietly walked down the short passage to his room. The door made no sound as it opened and she peeked inside. He slept on his stomach and his sheet was blinding white against his tanned lower back.

Clem stepped inside and looked around. Big black-framed, sepia-coloured and mesmerizing seascape photographs dominated the wall above his leather headboard. Three pillows had landed on the floor next to his boots and his black and white checked easy chair was draped with clothes.

Books and DVDs sat in wonky piles on the floor and his wallet, mobile, radio and keys were on his chest of drawers, along with a pair of pliers, a couple of electrical adapters, an iPod and a heart rate monitor.

He was still sound asleep. She fought the urge to slip out of her clothes and to climb into bed with him, to stroke her hands through that thick hair, down that long back, tracing the line of his spine. To wake him up with a hot kiss and insistent hands.

Concentrate, Clem, you're here to annoy him, not seduce him. So she banged the coffee cup down on his bedside table and whipped away to yank the curtains open.

'Get your lazy ass out of bed, Sherwood. You're going to be late!' Clem snapped, raising her voice and clapping her hands. 'You've got fifteen minutes or you go as you are.'

She bundled his mosquito net into a messy knot and bent down to yank his sheet away at the same time that Nick groaned and rolled over.

'Come on! Up! Up! Up!'

It took Clem ten seconds to realize that, unlike her, Nick did not sleep in pyjamas.

She looked down at his chest, lightly covered in hair, moved onto his six-pack stomach, then lower and...oh, dear God.

She came to her senses and slapped her hands onto her face, knowing that her entire body was blushing. 'Whaaaah!'

She heard the rustle of the sheet and Nick moving to, she presumed, sit up. 'Clem? What's the matter?'

She heard the amusement in his voice and blushed deeper. She looked for her tongue and managed to get it working. She turned her back to him, dropped her hands and stared at the floor. 'I was trying to wake you up, like you do me, and I...'

'You what?'

'Got distracted,' Clem muttered, utterly mortified. 'You sleep naked,' she whispered.

'Clearly.'

Clem took a step towards the door. 'I'll leave now...give you some privacy.'

'Bit late now, Red.'

Out of the corner of her eye she watched Nick stand up, stretch. He seemed utterly at ease in his skin. Clem caught a glimpse of those long thighs, a pale buttock as he walked into his en suite bathroom, and she seriously considered running after him and...

Oh dear. What the hell was she going to do?

CHAPTER FIVE

Luella Dawson's blog:

Clem's back! Thank the gods and goddesses of reality TV, who were torturing us with Cai and Kiki...

My little bird told me that Clem will take part in the second season of the CC's and filming is due to start at the Baobab and Buffalo Lodge and Rehabilitation Centre where Clem is working— that has to be wrong, Clem working? — as a trainee game ranger.

As I write this I'm thinking that maybe my little bird has fallen off his perch and knocked his head...none of this makes sense! But I write it as I hear it.

AT THE airstrip, Nick parked by the hangar and looked across at Clem, who was looking anywhere but at him. Nick grinned; she hadn't met his eyes since she'd left his bedroom that morning and he found it hysterically funny. Who would've thought that the society princess would feel so embarrassed at seeing a naked man? A fully—and, to be fair, aroused—naked man, but she didn't need to get her panties in a wad about it.

Nick rubbed his chin. As she stood up and hopped off the Landy, he wondered if she knew how close to the edge she'd pushed him this morning. He'd had to grip the sheets in an effort not to rear up and yank her down to the bed to join him.

He wanted her like he wanted to take his next breath.

'You're going to have to look at and talk to me some time.'

Clem stared at her feet, seemingly fascinated by her pretty pink toes. 'Does never work for you?'

'I've never seen anyone blush with their entire body before. Or turn that particular shade of pink,' Nick said conversationally, picking up his set of keys from the dashboard. He slipped his mobile into the pocket of his cream and rust untucked button-down shirt and shoved his sunglasses onto the top of his head. His radio went into the back pocket of his brown cargo shorts.

'Can we just not talk about it any more?' Clem asked.

Nick jerked his head for her to follow him to the hangar. 'I would like to say that, for the record, I think it's deeply unfair that you've see me in the buff but I've only seen you in your underwear.'

'Yeah, well, that's not going to change any time soon,' Clem said.

Oh, if they weren't very careful they both knew it could and would.

He'd had enough women to know that she liked the way he looked, that she wanted him as much as he wanted her. If she was just passing through, wasn't his partner's daughter, was fractionally less crazy he'd have had her already. But they had to work together, be together, have those cameras in their faces for the next two weeks.

All good and solid reasons for keeping his hands off her, but the most compelling reason he needed to keep his distance was due to the neon sign flashing behind his eyes.

Danger! Emotional curves and connections ahead. Proceed with extreme caution!

He'd navigated that corner before, lost control and tumbled down the cliff. He was not crazy, or stupid enough to repeat the experience. He wasn't that good a driver.

Nick pushed open the hangar doors and walked inside the

dark interior. On auto-pilot, he grabbed the aircraft tug, fitted it to the light aircraft and pulled it into the sunshine.

'Close the hangar doors,' he told Clem, who just stayed where she was, arms folded and looking at the sky. When he realized what she was waiting for, the corner of his mouth kicked up.

'Close the hangar doors, Red. Please.'

'Ah, so he does have a rudimentary concept of manners,' Clem said before swaggering away. She tossed a naughty grin at him over her shoulder.

'Pretty cocky for someone who was perving at me this morning,' Nick called after her.

Clem threw a look at him over her shoulder. If he didn't know better, he would've called it flirty. 'I was not perving!'

Nick laughed and banged his head against the door of his plane. 'Tell me again why you were in my room?'

Pushing the doors closed, Clem tapped her thigh with her finger and rocked on her heels. Embarrassment or lust? He couldn't be sure. A bit of both?

'I was trying to wake you up. Act like a jerk to show you what it feels like to be woken up by someone shouting at you.'

'Sounds like an excuse to take a look.' Nick watched as she leaned back against the plane and he moved so that he was standing in front of her, his hand on the frame behind her head. He looked at her mouth and remembered her taste. 'You could've just asked, you know.'

She dropped her head back in a move that was as natural as it was seductive and her hair glinted in the early morning sunshine. Gold and blonde and red and orange... He could count a hundred different shades.

'You have the most fantastic hair,' Nick quietly said, unable to stop his fingers from sliding into the curls, the tips of his fingers making circles on her scalp.

Clem licked her lips and Nick watched her eyes deepen and darken, felt her fingers reach up to encircle his wrist.

Nick stepped closer to her and rested his forehead against hers. 'We can't do this, Clementine.'

He felt her nod. 'I know.'

'I want to anyway,' Nick admitted. 'I want you but I don't want to want you.'

'Me too. You and I are exact opposites, from different worlds.' Clem's thumb brushed the inside of his wrist. 'We don't even like each other.'

'The real problem is this heat between us.'

Clem lifted her head and their eyes caught and held.

There it went.

Just like every time. When she looked at him like that— as if he was the one man who could ever, had ever made her react like this—the world receded and all the air was sucked out of his lungs. After an intense minute just staring at each other, Nick stepped back and Clem shoved a hand into that fabulous hair and lifted slim shoulders in a small shrug.

'Heat is not enough,' Nick muttered. 'Trust me, bitter experience has taught me this.'

'I'm not arguing with you,' Clem quietly replied but he could see the pulse in her neck hammering. 'But I still want you to kiss me. Sorry, but I do.'

The last time he checked, he wasn't a freaking saint... Oh, wait, he'd never been a saint or anything close to one so he gripped her wrist and pulled her towards him. He held her against him, on her toes, her body flat against his, his mouth a scant inch from hers. Nothing was important but this girl and her soft body and hot eyes.

Clem felt tension curl and swirl in her stomach, knew that she was about to lick her upper lip and couldn't help it... Her hips moved closer to his. Couldn't help that. His mouth opened and Clem waited in breathless anticipation. She knew what he wanted to say, to ask. Why did he even bother— surely he could see her answer in her eyes, on her face?

It's crazy and wild and I'll probably regret it but...yes, kiss me again, make me yours.

Like the last time they kissed, she expected him to swoop and devour, but his mouth was more gentle than she expected. He nibbled and explored and tempted. Clem's hands found their way to his back, up and under his shirt, to feel that hard, warm, male flesh...

'Nick, come in. Switch to channel thirteen.'

The radio in his back pocket squawked but Nick didn't release his grip on her when he lifted his head, flipped channels with one hand, brought the radio to his mouth and hit the call button to talk. 'Yeah, Jabu, what is it?'

'Bad time, *mfo*?'

You have no idea, Clem silently grumbled, her hands flat on Nick's muscled chest. She'd move but she wasn't sure if her legs would hold her yet. And whilst her libido was screaming for some more action, her head and her heart were on bended knees yelling, *Thank God you stopped! We're not ready!*

'What do you want, Jabu?' Nick muttered, his fingers dipping into the small gap between the band of her shorts and her warm skin, skimming over the T of her panties. His mouth dropped and he touched her lips with his.

'Nicholas!' Jabu's voice had Nick jerking back and scowling. 'Can you stop doing whatever you're doing for a minute and concentrate? This is important.'

Nick pulled his hand from her back and scratched his forehead. Clem, realizing that the moment was over, lifted her hands from his chest in a gesture of surrender and took a step back.

'What is it, Jabu?'

'Poachers dehorned a rhino cow on the reserve up north last night. One of ours.'

Nick's eyes flattened with fury and she immediately stepped back. He swore viciously and dropped to his haunches, his finger and thumb gripping the bridge of his nose.

'We're getting the rest of those rhinos off that property this week.' His voice was hard and Clem doubted that anyone, anywhere, would have the guts to disagree with him at that moment.

'That's the plan.' Jabu's voice sounded weary.

Nick stood up and placed his fist on his hip. 'Book the transport, the vet, the capture specialists. *Mfo*, we need to get those rhinos out of there.'

'The money? They'll all want some money upfront.'

'Hold on, I'll check.'

Nick looked at her and Clem nodded sombrely. 'I'll check with Jason, see that he's done the transfer. Do you...do you need more?'

Nick shook his head. 'The money won't be a problem, Jabu. Just get the ball rolling.'

'You got it,' Jabu replied, signing off.

Clem watched as a shudder passed through his body, then another and saw the turbulent emotions in his eyes. He looked past her and she knew that his brain was running at warp speed, fury and sadness bubbling under the surface.

Nick heaved in a huge breath and rubbed his temple before glancing at his watch and grimacing. 'The worst way to start the day. We've got to get going.'

He pulled open the front passenger door and gestured her to climb inside. 'I'm going to do my pre-flight checks. I won't be too long.'

Clem watched him walk around the plane and squirmed in her seat. He was such a fascinating mix of hard male strength and capability but, when it came to his land or his animals, he had a kernel of vulnerability that touched her. And whenever he physically laid hands on her he made her blood sing.

This could become very complicated, she thought ruefully.

* * *

The sky was a beautiful concoction of blues and the sun a broad golden band on the horizon when Nick pulled into the air and cleared the trees at the end of the runway. Clem watched as he fiddled with the controls as the plane gained altitude and speed. When, she presumed, he was at the right altitude and on course for the airport at the regional capital of Mbombela, he leaned back in his seat and turned his head to look at her.

'You OK?' he asked.

His voice was warm and sexy in her ears, deep and dark through the headset. She felt as if he was speaking directly to her soul.

'I'm fine.' Clem turned in her seat and rested her head on the back of her seat. 'We need to talk about the filming. Jason sent me an e-mail confirming that they are doing a run-and-gun shoot with us, partly because you said that there's no space for a big crew.'

'Two people, that's it. What is a run-and-gun shoot?'

'Basically, it's them following the action. They won't have a coverage plan, they just want interesting, fun stuff and it's up to us to provide it for them.'

'Define interesting or fun,' Nick said.

Clem shrugged. 'It could be lots of things. Conflict and fights provides a lot of entertainment. So does sex and intrigue. None of that will work for us, so I've been thinking about how to give them what they want so that they don't have to splice and dice and make a story.'

'Uh huh?'

'As much as I hate to admit this, the audience will enjoy seeing me in situations that I feel uncomfortable in. The dirtier and yuckier the better.'

Nick's white teeth flashed. 'Back to recycling for you, Princess.'

'Ha ha...no. Every morning you and I have to work out a bit of a schedule, what I'm going to do, how I'm going to do it. We've got to control what they see and hear so you've got to remember that we're on camera so you can't say anything stupid. They will not edit it out.' Clem lifted a warning finger. 'And no touching or kissing or anything like that. They'll lap that up.'

'Dang, here I thought we were going to get all hot and heavy on screen.' Nick's irreverent reply was accompanied by a wicked grin.

Clem thought he was taking this whole concept a lot better than she'd expected so she ploughed on. 'And then we've got to remember that we're trying to raise money for your foundation so we need to get footage of me working in the sanctuary, on game drives, on horseback...'

Clem dropped a hand into the cooler between the seats to pull out a bottle of water. Nick's hand brushed hers as he took the bottle from her grasp, cracked the top and handed it back to her. Clem sipped and lubricated her dry mouth and throat. She was so close to him she could feel the heat of his body, with every breath she inhaled his scent... Citrusy with something masculine and indefinable—primal—beneath.

Clem's riotous thoughts were interrupted by Nick swearing. She leaned forward in her seat. 'What's wrong; why are you saying that?'

Nick pointed to a massive build-up of clouds in the distance. 'Sorry, no need to panic. Nothing is wrong with the plane. I'm looking at those clouds. They are too far away from Two-B... We need the rain.'

Clem relaxed back into her seat as Nick spoke again. 'At this rate, Jabu and I are going to have to do our rain dance.'

Clem lifted one eyebrow. 'Your what?'

Nick grinned. 'We used to do it when we were kids, thought that the Rain Goddess would listen if we pranced naked around a fire.'

'I would pay good money to see that.'

'Well, you got a preview this morning. And she blushes

again! Your face, neck, shoulders...' Nick turned, leaned forward and with one finger pulled her shirt away from her chest. 'Yep, right down to your bra.'

Clem slapped his hand away, groaned and dropped her head to her knees. 'Am I ever going to live this down?'

'Not in this lifetime.'

'Red? You OK?' Nick pushed open the door to Clem's room, wondering if she was sleeping through this humdinger of a storm, dead to the world. The lights had gone out a while ago and lightning zzzed and jabbed all around them and thunder rolled and roared.

Waiting for the next lightning strike to light up the room, he frowned when he saw her bed was empty.

'Clem?'

Nick stepped into the room and his heart clenched when he saw her on the floor, knees to her chest and her arms over her head. Crouching down in front of her, he placed a hand on her head and another on her shoulder. 'It's just a storm, Clem.'

Terrified eyes looked at him from a pale, bloodless face. She was scared down to her soul, Nick realized. Lifting her hands off her head, he pulled her arms around his neck and scooped her up.

'Let's go to my room, I've got a lamp burning.'

Another flash of lightning had Clem jumping in his arms as he maneuvred her into the passage and, pushing open his door with his foot, walked with her into his room.

He pulled back the sheet and thin bedspread on the other side of his bed and placed her inside the covers, pulling the sheet over her shoulders when he noticed the fine tremors running through her body. He looked at the curtains billowing in the wind and shook his head... Thunder and lightning was one thing but they needed the heavy drops, the pounding fury of a violent summer storm.

He looked over to Clem, curled up in his bed, her eyes screwed shut.

Why was he so focused on this woman? Normal women were difficult enough to figure out, but this one was the biggest, craziest complication he'd ever come across. She was his chief investor's darling daughter, lived a life that kept magazines and tabloid newspapers churning and was, basically, a royal pain in his butt.

He hated the fact that he found Clem intriguing...but there was something about her that made him want to scratch below the surface. Why was she so terrified of thunderstorms? What was it like growing up with an icon for a mother? Did she have a good relationship with her father? He understood that she'd just come out of a long term relationship but he sensed that the lost, desperate look in her eyes had been there for a long, long time.

Thinking like this was dangerous, Nick reminded himself. It made it harder to be sensible, to stay mentally uninvolved, to keep his barriers impenetrable.

He'd made the right decision years ago to keep his relationships with women—hell, with people, family—devoid of emotion. He'd been surrounded by passionate, emotional people all his life and, even when he'd—subconsciously—chosen a self-reliant, undramatic and seemingly dispassionate woman for a wife, his marriage had ended in a mess of all the seething, complicated feelings he'd tried to run away from.

Yet, for some weird reason, Clem's arrival had put those unwelcome feelings back on to simmer.

She flung her arms over her head and screamed into the mattress as another lightning strike hit the hill behind them. Sighing, Nick walked to the bed and lay behind her, his arm protectively wrapped around her waist.

It wasn't until the thunder faded and heavy raindrops bounced off the roof that Clem slept, with her hand holding his hand against her heart.

* * *

For once, Clem woke up before Nick. She slipped out from under that broad hand on her hip and, after she'd returned from the bathroom, she curled up into his easy chair and watched him sleep.

She'd made a grave error by assuming that he wouldn't check on her during the storm and she was mortified that he'd found her, whimpering like a fool, huddled in a corner. She should've known that he was a protector, he did it so naturally and his basic instinct was to look after the well being of all living creatures on his land.

That seemed to include her.

She hated storms. She didn't know if she'd have been able to get through it without Nick—literally—having her back. But she'd revealed too much of herself and, while he hadn't asked for any explanations, she knew he'd be curious about her phobia. And, strangely, she felt herself wanting to tell him, to explain why she associated lightning and thunder with the most devastating time of her life.

He'd understand, she was sure of it. She suspected that he had a well tuned emotional antenna beneath that obvious I-am-happy-alone personality. He was, Clem admitted, the most self-sufficient person she'd ever come across and she found that trait of his personality deeply attractive.

Possibly because she was such a tangle of insecurity herself, not being sure if she'd ever been unconditionally loved, even by her parents. Clem winced. That reeked of self-pity but it didn't make it less true. They had been few, if any, words of love and their actions had spoken loudly.

Her mum's litany of broken promises ranged from missing dinners to dance recitals and graduation ceremonies. There had always been something so much more important to do—a story to cover, a discussion in parliament to attend, a report to write.

Her father hadn't been any better. How nice if would've been if he'd arrived with the jet to take her from New York to Nick's, providing physical and mental support instead of just a means of transport and a place to hide out. But he'd been in sensitive negotiations and couldn't leave.

There were always sensitive negotiations on a deal that couldn't be left.

Maybe that was why she so badly wanted a child. Someone to give her unconditional love to, someone to love her back. Maybe then the emptiness inside would go away.

'You're a bed hogger,' Nick said and she snapped her head up. How long had he been leaning on his elbows, watching her?

'A what?'

'You hog the bed like a starfish. Good thing we're not sleeping together because that would be a deal breaker.'

'Hey guys, where are you?' Mdu shouted and Clem bolted upright.

'Are they supposed to be filming so early? How did they get here?' She kept her voice low. 'What are we going to do? If they find me in here they are going to think that I'm sleeping with you!'

Nick looked from her to the bed and back again and she threw a pillow at his head, secretly grateful for an excuse to avoid any awkward morning-after discussions. 'Nick!'

'Thinking, thinking...'

CHAPTER SIX

Luella Dawson's blog:

> *OMG, did you enjoy the first episode of Clem's crazy adventure as much as I did? Love her hair, by the way, and do you think she's picked a smidgeon of weight?*
>
> *But double OMG, what do you think about the luscious Nick? Two words: Yum and Mee! Beneath their snappy conversation, sparks are leaping; did you notice him checking out her legs? And she sends him these little sidelong glances when she thinks he's not looking. I think something is cooking, folks!*

THIRTY minutes later, after boosting Clem over the wall that separated their outdoor showers, Nick was scrambling eggs for breakfast. He swallowed when Clem walked into the kitchen, dressed in a pair of khaki shorts, a Two-B golf shirt and the dusty hiking boots he'd found for her in the uniform store.

He thought he'd never seen anything sexier in his life. She looked fresh and young, less like the cosmopolitan heiress than ever, and a far cry from the vulnerable girl of last night. Because his heart stumbled and fell over his feet, his voice came out clipped. 'Boots fit?'

Clem looked down and shook her head in horror. 'Yes, but

have you ever seen anything uglier? Good grief, if there was an award for ugly shoes, these would win.'

Nick tugged her hair as she walked past. 'You'll think they are great if you get tagged on the foot by a puff adder.'

Nick narrowed his eyes as he noticed Mdu trailing the camera down and then up Clem's legs.

'OK, you win the "reason to wear ugly boots" argument.' Clem grabbed a cup from above the kettle and rammed it under the spout of his coffee machine. While she waited for it to dispense, she looked around Nick at the eggs in the pan.

Nick's mobile rang and Clem picked it up and waved it in his direction. 'Your mother.'

Nick shook his head. 'Let it go to message.'

Clem frowned. 'You don't take calls from your mother? Why not?'

'I do take calls from her,' Nick protested and, seeing her disbelieving look, shrugged. 'Sometimes, OK...rarely. She's...'

'Mmm?'

Nick pushed the eggs around in the pan. 'I have four siblings and everyone in my family is excitable and loud and feels the need to know the intimate details of my life.'

'And you are reticent and reserved and independent.'

'Sometimes living with them felt like I was living in a soap opera. Drama, drama, drama.'

Mdu bumped a chair and Nick grimaced, suddenly reminded of the cameras in the room. He sent Mdu a measured glance. 'Erase that, please.'

Mdu nodded at the command in his voice. 'Sure. No problem.'

Clem nodded at the stove. 'Why are you cooking breakfast? Why aren't we eating at the canteen?'

Nick stirred the eggs and put bread in the toaster. 'No time. I need to get you to work at the animal sanctuary and then I have to get back to take a conference call about the ball.'

Clem perked up. 'Ball? What ball?'

Nick took her cup from her hands, took a sip and asked her to make him one. As Clem reached for another cup, he filled her in. 'It's a fund-raising event for my foundation. My marketing company got a multinational to sponsor the event so all the money from ticket sales goes to the foundation. There's also an auction at the end of it.'

'When's the ball?'

'A few weeks' time. Want to go?'

'Seriously?'

Nick shrugged. 'I should take a partner and you're as good as any.' He flashed a smile at her. 'Being marginally attractive and all that.'

Clem's fingers fluttered above her heart. 'I don't think I've had a more gracious invitation in my life. Thank you so much!' she gushed.

Nick's lips lifted. 'Wiseass.'

He dished the eggs up onto plates. 'On a related subject, Andy—one of my senior game rangers—is having his birthday party at The Pit tonight. He's from America's Mid-west and he's determined to teach everyone line dancing. Do you line dance?'

'I took dance lessons from the age of three to fifteen. There's not much I can't do,' Clem replied as she put sugar into Nick's cup of black coffee and stirred it for him. 'Oh, that sounds like so much fun. Can we go?'

'Thanks.' Nick took the cup she held out, sipped and sighed with pleasure. 'Well, you can, I need to eat up at the Lodge with the guests tonight. I'll meet you at The Pit later.'

Clem grinned as she took Nick's coffee cup to the dining table for him, while he handed Liam and Mdu their plates. 'Woo-hoo. A party! And I cleaned The Pit yesterday so I know I don't need a tetanus shot!'

* * *

Nick got to The Pit around eleven and the party was in full swing. He noticed that about a dozen dancers were doing something very complicated on the far side of the room, which had been turned into a dance floor for the evening. He couldn't see Clem and lifted his eyebrows at Jabu, who had his elbow on the bar and a beer in his hand.

'Hey.' Jabu lifted his bottle and signalled the bartender for another for Nick.

'Hey back.' Nick stood next to him and looked over the crowded bar. 'Looks like a great party!'

'Red and Hannah are in the middle of the action,' Jabu replied and handed Nick the beer the bartender slid over the counter.

'Where are they?' Nick lifted his bottle to his mouth and stopped halfway. The two lines of dancers turned to face them and there she was, laughing with Jabu's wife, Hannah. While Hannah was dressed in a denim skirt and T-shirt, Clem had taken the cowboy theme to the limit.

She was wearing another pair of short, short denim shorts, an open neck sleeveless white shirt that she'd tied under her breasts and cowboy boots.

God knew where she'd found the cowboy hat but, since anything was possible with Clem, she could have brought it with her in one of her numerous suitcases.

Nick took a deep sip of his beer and wasn't thrilled to realize that every male eye in the bar was watching those legs, those swaying hips, toes and heels clicking, long legs flashing.

'She's been hitting the punch pretty hard,' Jabu told him and Nick looked at him, horrified.

'What punch?'

'Andy made punch for the kids. After they left, he chucked in a bottle of vodka.'

Nick winced. 'She doesn't drink alcohol.'

Jabu looked horrified and Nick lifted a hand. 'No, she's not an alcoholic; she just doesn't drink.'

'Well, she's been pouring the punch down her throat like it's juice,' Jabu told him as the song came to an end.

'This is going to be interesting,' Nick commented as Clem and Hannah walked towards them, arm in arm.

'Nick! You're here!' Clem shouted and broke into an on-the-spot boogie.

Nick slanted a look at Jabu. 'As I said. Interesting.'

'Look at me! I'm dancing!' Clem grinned and attempted to do a pirouette. Nick's hand shot out and gripped her elbow and kept her from falling flat on her face.

'I see that.' Nick pulled her to his side and wrapped a hand around her waist.

Clem rested her head on his shoulder. 'I love dancing and it's one of the few things I'm really, really good at. I'm also good at knitting!'

Nick laughed. 'Knitting?'

'I took a course. I've taken lots of courses.'

'Uh-huh.' Nick sipped his beer and grinned at her squinting eyes. Keeping his firm hold on Clem, he reached forward to kiss Hannah. 'Hey, gorgeous. Looking good out there.'

Hannah put her hand on his cheek and patted it. 'Such fun. You two should try it.'

'When I can snowboard in hell,' Nick replied.

'Hey!' Clem protested and leaned back in his arm. Nick turned his head to look into her affronted face. 'How come she gets a kiss and I don't?'

'Oh boy. How much of that punch did you drink, Red?'

'Losth.' Clem looked as if she was about to impart a huge secret. 'I think there was something in it.'

Nick laughed. 'You think?'

Clem dazzled him with one of her mega-watt smiles. 'Nick, you still haven't kissed me!'

'Uh—' Nick felt her hands reach up to squish his cheeks together. Fish face, he thought as she planted one on him before pulling back. She still held his face in her hands when

she cocked her head and contemplated him with those amazing eyes. 'I really like kissing you.'

He heard Jabu and Hannah's smothered laughter and
winced. 'Clem, I think we need to get you home...'

'He's a great kisser,' Clem told Hannah.

'Good to know.' Hannah's dimples flashed. 'I think that's
a great trait in a man.'

'Nice hands, too.'

'I wondered...'

'Hey!' Jabu mock complained, laughter in his voice. 'What
else, Clem?'

Nick glowered at his friends. 'Stop encouraging her!'

Clem cocked her head but didn't let go of his face. 'I love
your eyes...moonlight eyes.'

Nick shot Jabu and Hannah, a *Rescue me!* look but they
both just smiled.

Nick pulled her hands down and held them loosely in his.
He wiggled his jaw to get the blood back to his lips. 'Thanks.'

The music on the stereo system changed, the volume in-
creased and Clem shot out of his arms like a bullet. Nick
watched as she headed straight for the dance floor and happily accepted, and downed, the glass of punch Andy held
out to her. When it was finished, he took the glass from her,
placed it on a table and hustled her into a complicated dance
that involved him holding her tight against his chest and his
jeaned leg sliding between hers.

Uh...no. That so wasn't happening.

Nick slapped his half finished beer on the bar and walked
over to the dance floor. Andy took one look at his face and,
quickly reading the situation, allowed Clem to spin into his
arms. He caught her and she grinned up at him.

'You're dancing with me!' Clem cried.

'You, Princess, are drunk. We're going home.'

'Don't want to!' Clem cried and shoved out her bottom lip.
She tried to step away but Nick held her wrist in his hand.

Clem tried to pull her hand away. 'Andy will dance with me if you won't.'

'Andy likes his job too much,' Nick muttered. 'We're going home.'

'Not!'

He was tired, dead sober and he didn't feel like having a scene in front of his staff. He needed to get her out of The Pit in the quickest and cleanest way possible. Arguing with her wasn't going to get him anywhere; Clem, he was learning, had the stubbornness of a mule.

So, quickest and easiest...Nick bent, grabbed Clem around the knees, lifted her and tossed her over his shoulder. Ignoring the catcalls and whistles and Clem's squawking, he held her legs and walked out of The Pit.

At the door, Andy whipped the Stetson off her head and planted it back on his. 'My hat. 'Night, boss.'

Nick grinned as he tipped her into the passenger seat of his Landy. Well, he couldn't say that he was bored.

'Ow! Ow, ow, ow!' Clem yelled as her bottom connected with the spring.

'Come on, Red, let's get you into bed.'

And I'm now a poet, Nick thought as he slid his arms under Clem's still far too skinny frame and cradled her like a baby. At the door to his house, he rested her on his raised knee, flipped the door open and manoeuvred her down the passage.

'You need some meat on your bones, Clementine,' he muttered.

'Don't break my heart, my achy breaky heart...' Clem sang into his neck and he grinned. She was off-key and squawky and couldn't hold a tune to save her life.

Nick nudged her door open and walked her to the double bed, pulling back the covers and laying her on a cool sheet. She immediately rolled onto her side and cradled her pillow.

'You can't sleep in your cowboy boots, Red,' Nick said,

bending to yank off one boot and then the other, dropping them to the floor. He worked her socks off, cradling her pretty pale feet in his hard tanned hand.

'Nick?'

'Mmm?' Nick sat on the side of her bed and pushed her hair off her cheek.

'It's been a long time since someone looked after me,' Clem said softly. 'It's nice. Do I hear thunder?'

'Storm's on its way.' Nick pushed her back as she tried to sit up. Clem put her head on the crisp pillow and reached for his hand. Nick allowed her to tangle her fingers in his.

'I need to say something to you.'

'OK.'

Clem's thumb drifted over his knuckles in a gesture that was as arousing as it was tender. Nick licked his lips. He knew how to do seduction, fast, hot sex, but he didn't know how to handle tenderness.

'When I arrived at Two-B, I acted like a brat.'

Nick tried to keep from smiling. Now there was an understatement. 'I know. It's OK.'

Clem shook her head. 'No, that's just part of what I want to say. I was a brat because I was scared. I always act badly when I'm scared. You scared me.'

'I scared you?' Nick asked, puzzled. That was the last thing he'd expected her to say.

'Mmm. You, this land…your stupid Landy. It was all so different, so…alien. You were so offhand and unimpressed with me…'

Unimpressed? Was she mad? He'd felt as if he'd been flattened by a tornado. It had taken all his effort not to fall at her feet and whimper.

Thankfully, Clem had absolutely no idea of the power of her body, face and voice. Teamed with her sparky humour and a surprisingly big heart, she was enough to induce an emotional heart attack.

'I didn't know how to behave and I was so, so scared… Everything was changing and change is scary. And you know what else?'

Those eyes just killed him. Soft, affectionate, vulnerable. 'What, sweetheart?'

'I'm not so scared any more.'

'Good girl.' Nick pushed her hair behind her ear and raised her hand to kiss her knuckles, keeping his eyes lowered so that she didn't see the emotion in his. 'There's nothing to be scared of… Life has its way of working out.'

A drum roll of thunder had Clem bolting upwards and scuttling towards Nick. He gathered her into his arms and moved so that he was leaning against the leather headboard, Clem tucked into his side. Toeing his shoes off, he lifted his feet onto the bed. He heard lightning sizzle.

'Thunder incoming,' he warned and when the noise subsided he asked his question in the most matter of fact voice he could find. 'Why do storms scare you, Clem?'

'My mum died in a thunderstorm. She'd just picked me up from ballet and we were hit by a truck and we spun and spun and I remember catching glimpses of her face in the lightning, knowing that she was gone. When we stopped, there was this most enormous clap of thunder…and I just screamed and screamed…'

'Shh, sweetheart.' Nick cursed when another slap of thunder rolled through the house. Oh, hell. She'd been fifteen years old and she'd watched her mum die in a storm… He'd hate thunder and lightning as well.

Poor kid. Clem slapped her hands to her ears so Nick put both his arms around her and held on tight, running his hands up her back to keep the shakes at bay.

'I've never known storms like this,' Clem whispered.

'Yeah, they can be pretty vicious. You're safe, sweetheart. Promise.'

'I still see her face... We'd just had a fight, about the fact that she was an hour late to collect me. She was always late...'

At that moment it seemed vitally important to pull her out of that memory so, operating on instinct, he bent down and kissed her, hoping to distract her.

Except that it was he who found himself swept away, lost in the moment. She tasted so sweet, soft as her arms drifted up to settle around his neck and her fingers played with his hair. She pulled away from the kiss and her eyes were deep and mysterious when she looked up at him. 'I like that I can be myself with you.'

'Good.'

'And that you don't sulk.'

Nick brushed his thumb over her cheekbone. 'You should see me when I don't get to hold the TV remote.'

'You're strong and sensible and you have nice hands,' Clem whispered. 'And I like the way you kiss.' She yawned and glanced towards the window and the billowing curtains. The sudden sound of rain hitting the roof filled the room.

Clem yawned. 'Rain's here.'

'Mmm.'

'I'll be OK 'cos you're here. 'Night.'

Nick watched her eyes close and within seconds she was asleep. He kissed her forehead, her cheek and then her mouth. 'Night, sweetheart.'

Nick felt her slump against him and gently banged his head against the headboard. He could handle bratty Clem and smart-mouth Clem and even flirty Clem, but sweet, soft, vulnerable Clem had the ability to wiggle her way into his heart.

Sweet Clem was far, far more dangerous than Sexy Clem could ever be.

It was sheer coincidence that Clem's godmother and her family were spending a week at the private villa during Clem's stay at Two-B and Clem and Nick accepted Gina's invitation to dinner at the villa a few days after Andy's party. After a gourmet meal from the private chef, Clem took her coffee and sat next to Gina on one of the three couches on the veranda. She looked past Gina and saw that Nick was sitting next to Fabio and they were looking at something on Fabio's laptop.

Gina held her cognac glass with one hand and took Clem's hand with her other. 'You're looking better. Not so unhappy, not so haunted.'

Darling Gina, so upfront and in your face. Clem leaned back, crossed her legs and blew out her cheeks. 'I know. I feel...I feel like I'm coming back to me.'

'Tell me more.'

Clem tried to find a way to describe how she was feeling. 'Um...the best way to explain it is that it's almost like being on a long trip with an old friend who I haven't seen for years and I'm getting to know her again.'

'And that's a good thing?'

'It's a very good thing.' Clem smiled.

'And are you a little in love?' Gina asked, sending a sly glance into the house.

Clem shook her head. 'I can't afford to think like that, Gee. I don't know me, so how can I know what I'm feeling towards someone else?'

Gina placed her cognac on the table next to her and leaned forward, her face serious. 'I'm glad you've left Cai; he was no good for you.'

Clem tapped her fingernail against her coffee cup. 'Funny that I've hardly thought about him, but I have been thinking about Mum a lot lately. That so much has been expected of me from so many people—teachers, the press, my parents— because of my genes. And that I've disgraced her memory.'

Gina's hand gripped hers and her eyes flashed with temper. 'You are *not* your mother, Clem, so don't you dare say that!'

'Oh, Gee, thank you, but the reality is that I've made a pig's ear of my life.'

'But it's your life to make a pig's ear of!' Gina pursed her lips. 'I loved Roz deeply but she failed you.'

'Excuse me?'

'When you have a child you've got to accept that your life will change, that this little person will come first. Roz never got that and you suffered for it. She loved you, I know she did, as much as she could, but…it was never enough for you.'

Clem blinked back her tears. 'No, it was never enough for me. I have an emptiness inside…I can't explain it.'

'It'll go when you accept that her not being the mother you needed was her failing and not yours.'

'Oh, Gee, you always know exactly the right thing to say.' Clem placed her head on her godmother's shoulder. Her eyes drifted to Nick, to find him looking at her, a concerned look on his face.

'Are you OK?' he mouthed.

Clem nodded.

Gina patted her thigh. 'I hope you've never doubted how much I love you.'

'No, I've never doubted that. You've been a rock throughout my life. I'm sorry I didn't make a bigger effort to see you.'

'I expect you to do better in the future. I do like that young man,' she commented as Nick stood up to walk over to them.

'Me too,' Clem sighed.

Nick joined them and Clem looked at her watch. 'We must go, Gina.'

'So early!'

Nick took Gina's hand and she stood up.

'Thank you for a fabulous evening. I understand that you are scheduled to take a game drive in the morning,' he said, holding her hand in his.

'With Siya. Such a nice, knowledgeable young man.'

'I'm glad to hear it, but would you settle for an older, slightly more knowledgeable man? One of my rangers in the anti-poaching unit is coming down with flu. I need to replace him with somebody else.'

Nick jammed his hands in his pockets. 'So, if you'd like to come with Clem and me, I'll show you a bit of the reserve that's off the beaten track.'

He was met with a chorus of excited Italian babbling. Nick held up his hand. 'We'll have the camera crew along and, I have to warn you, it's a pretty early start.'

Clem sighed and yawned. 'Is there any other type of start with you?'

Nick opened the door and gestured Clem inside. Walking inside the house, he heard the rumble of thunder and saw Clem stiffen. 'It's miles away, Red.'

Clem pushed her hair off her face and managed a smile. 'I'm sorry if you were bored to tears tonight; nothing is worse than sitting through hours of family memories.'

'Wasn't bored,' Nick replied, leaning against the wall, watching her. Clem toed the tiled floor with the tip of her shoe and recognized the look on his face, sure that hers was exactly the same. She wanted—no, needed—to feel those arms around her, her lips under his.

They'd been watching each other all night, and sitting next to each other at dinner had been exquisite torture. A brush of his shoulder against hers, his hand resting along the back of her chair, fingers occasionally and lightly brushing her back. The flash of citrusy aftershave when he'd said something in her ear, his foot hooked behind hers...

She hadn't been much better. They'd danced around each other all night with hot glances, secret smiles and brief touches until she felt like the lead in a romantic comedy.

'So, are you coming to me or am I coming to you?' Nick quietly asked.

Her eyes slammed into his and they both moved. Nick's

hard mouth dropped over hers and his tall, muscular frame held hers against the wall as his mouth dominated hers.

Clem whimpered in his mouth, hooked her hands around his neck and boosted herself up, her legs anchored around his waist. Nick held her easily and Clem felt his corresponding flash of lust shoot through him as she angled her head to allow him deeper access. It was different from the kiss they'd shared previously; it was...more. Harder, deeper, hotter. As he moved to sit her on the dining room table, she wasn't sure where she started and he ended, they were such a knot of need, passion and sheer frustration. Hands travelled and touched, silently seeking and demanding, sliding and drifting. His lips explored, nuzzled, nipped, tasted, creating a hyper-awareness of her body.

It was as if he'd plugged her into a bolt of lightning and she thought that maybe here was a storm she could handle.

'Nick...' Clem wasn't sure if she begged him to stop the torture or to increase the pleasure as he ravished her.

He wasn't going to be able to stop this, Nick thought as those slim fingers skated over his stomach. She was on fire for him... He could feel her ragged breathing in his ear, the way her fingers convulsively dug into his skin, the arch of her back.

Nick felt her fingers tug at the waistband of his trousers, felt her fingers slide behind the band...damn it, that was cold! And sharp. Nick lifted his head and pulled back and lifted her left hand. Her ring sparkled coldly up at him, mocking him in the moonlight as his thumb rested on the big diamond.

'Nick—'

He stepped back and heaved in a much needed breath. Damn it, why did it feel as if the air held no oxygen? 'I can't do this.'

Clem nodded. 'It's—'

'It's a whacking diamond, still on your ring finger. Something you're obviously attached to, which makes me wonder how much you are still attached to the person who gave you that ring.' Nick raked his hair back.

'I'm not—'

Sleeping with her would be a mistake. He knew this as well as he knew the Two-B land. Unlike the women who'd ambled in and out of his life before, Clem was wiggling her way into places in his heart and mind that had been long closed up. If he slept with her he might as well just open the damn stable door and let the horse bolt away with his heart.

Not an experience he was keen to repeat.

Clem gnawed her bottom lip. 'I'm not married, Nick. I can do this.'

Nick shook his head. 'There are more types of marriage than ones signed by a judge or priest, Red. If I have you, then I don't want anyone else in the room with us...'

'He's not... You don't understand.'

'If that was true, then you sure as hell wouldn't be wearing his ring.' Nick ignored her outburst. 'I was married so I know what it's like trying to move on when a part of you wants to stay there. But the thing is, Red, I was a third wheel in my own marriage. I'm not into threesomes, sexually or emotionally.'

Well, hell, where had that come from? He'd had no intention of telling her that he'd once been hitched.

And there was another reason why he should keep his distance from her, Nick thought as he walked to his own room. Her eyes were like a truth drug... She just looked at him and the words bubbled out.

Well, hell. Again.

CHAPTER SEVEN

Luella Dawson's blog:

> *It's official, I'm in love. In love with Nick, in love with his stunning Lodge—no, they aren't allowed to film it but I did look at his website—in love with his land!*
>
> *And weirdly, sort of in love with this new Clem. Oh, she's useless but you've got to admit that she's working her tail off.*

AFTER promising to visit Gina and her family again before they left Two-B, Clem gave them all a last hug and climbed back into the game viewing vehicle with Nick and his sick ranger. Clem sent the man a worried look; his face was grey-black and he was shaking with fever.

Summer flu, Clem thought; there was nothing worse.

Oh wait, there was something worse…Nick giving her the silent treatment. He'd barely exchanged more than a couple of words with her all morning, not even to argue with her. Clem lifted her hand up and instinctively clutched the locket around her neck. She'd slipped it on this morning, as she always did when she was feeling a little lost and a lot alone. It always gave her a sense of connection to her mum, one she'd never felt when she was alive.

Clem looked down at her now ringless hand and sighed.

Cai had given her the diamond for her twenty-first birthday and it was such a part of her that she'd genuinely forgotten about it. She'd never, in a million years, thought than Nick would associate it with marriage or think that she could still be attached to that…cretin.

She'd just assumed that he knew that she was very over Cai.

Clem looked at Nick's hard face, his eyes covered by his sunglasses. 'Cai means nothing to me…you've got to believe that.'

Nick flicked her a warning glance. 'Cameras.'

Clem sighed. She'd forgotten; thank goodness one of them was thinking straight. She needed to take a step back anyway, to try and work out what she was feeling for this man. She'd always been impulsive, plunging head-first into situations and then, finding she was floundering, her pride and her stubbornness kicked in and kept her rooted in the situation she'd tumbled into.

Maybe it was time to think before she leapt. Despite what Nick believed, she was over Cai, so very done with him. But she still had to figure out who she was, what she wanted, where she was going…

Work out her mummy issues.

And, as much as it shamed her, she liked having an excuse to pull back from Nick, she admitted. The feelings he brought to the surface in her were huge, consuming, frightening.

Sexy, strong, reliable, honest. Tough and full of integrity. Nick worked at something that mattered, that made a difference. She admired that, she admired him, she could probably, if she let herself, fall in love with him.

But she couldn't think of being in any type of a relationship with her life in such a state of flux. That was stupid and wasn't she done with being stupid?

Clem was jerked out of her musings by Nick braking and Clem looked at him as he stopped the vehicle.

'What's the matter?'

'Can you hear anything?'

'I'm not sure what I should be listening for.'

'There it is again.' Nick floored the accelerator and pulled off into the bush, directing the vehicle between two thorn bushes. 'I think it's coming from over there.'

'Over there', Clem realized, turned out to be a mud hole, and Nick took the vehicle as close to the mud as he could, stood behind the wheel and scanned the pan and the surrounding bush. Clem stood up as well and echoed his actions, not having any idea what she was doing. 'What are we looking for?'

Nick muttered a string of obscenities and pointed at the pan. 'That.'

Clem looked to where he was pointing and shook her head. All she could see was brown-grey mud... Wait, were those ears she saw twitching? 'It's a baby rhino, stuck in the mud. Oh, no, Nick!'

Nick jumped out of the vehicle and walked to the edge of the mud hole. 'It's tiny—three, four weeks old.' He turned back and looked at Bayanda, who was slumped over the edge of the vehicle. 'I need to see if I can get it out. Can you cover me? The mother might still be around...'

Bayanda stood up, lifted the rifle to his shoulder and nodded. 'I'll cover you.'

Clem grabbed Nick's arm as he walked past her. 'Nick, be careful.'

Nick sent her a grim smile, stripped off his boots and socks and walked into the mud. Clem watched as he made his way to the rhino, whose legs were deeply embedded in the mud. Its bleating was becoming progressively weaker. Clem looked around, keeping an eye out for the mummy rhino, but her eyes were drawn back to Nick, who grabbed the little rhino by its ears and tugged. She could see his muscles straining but the animal didn't move an inch in the sticky mud.

She knew that Nick was cursing, could see his lips moving as he tried to budge the calf. After a couple of minutes, he straightened and shouted to Clem, 'Call Jabu on the radio, tell him the situation and to round up whoever is available and get them here.'

Clem did as he asked and when she signed off, she jumped off the vehicle and pulled off her boots and socks. She followed Nick's path into the mud and immediately felt her feet sink, wet, slimy mud creeping up between her toes and up her bare legs. Gross. Did snakes live in mud? Scorpions? Even leeches? She fought the urge to scuttle away but pressed on forward. By the time she reached Nick, she was up to her knees and battling to move.

She placed a hand on Nick's shoulder, looking at the little calf, whose breathing was laboured. 'What do you want me to do?'

'I don't know if it's going to make it. It's so weak.' Nick, breathing heavily, pushed back his hair with his wrist.

'How long do you think it's been in here?'

'Since yesterday, at the very least. Its mother would've spent the night chasing off predators but she's probably abandoned it by now. She might still be hanging around; that's why I've got Bayanda covering us.' Nick blew out a breath. 'Will you help me pull?'

'Sure.'

'Grab the ears,' Nick instructed. 'Don't worry about hurting it, just get a good grip and pull.'

Clem wrapped her hands around the rhino's ears and added her strength to Nick's but the animal did not move. Clem gasped for air.

Nick shook his head. 'This isn't working.'

'Am I'm sinking further into the mud,' Clem said, noticing that she was now in mud up to her thighs.

'Yeah, I'm also sinking.' Nick rested his hands on his thighs. 'She's stopped crying; that isn't a good sign.'

Clem placed muddy hands on her hips and then swatted a fly that landed on her neck. 'Plan B?'

'Thinking.' Nick moved to the side of the rhino and felt in the mud for its legs. 'OK, what we need to do is grab the front legs, lift and push it forward at the same time. Can you do that?'

Clem waded her way to the other side of the tiny calf. Her eyes met his across the rhino's back. 'Yes. We are *not* losing this animal, Nick.'

'Good girl. Get your hands on the leg, put your shoulder to its shoulder and, on three, you lift and shove.'

Clem crouched, got as good a grip as she could on its leg and waited for Nick's instruction. She dimly heard the sound of another vehicle pulling up but all her concentration was focused on Nick's voice and, as he said 'Go,' she put every ounce of strength she had into lifting and pushing. Her arms and legs were on fire and she could barely breathe but she wasn't giving up. Just when she thought she'd pass out with the strain, she heard a *pop!* and the weight was lifted as the calf found solid ground, wobbled and walked out of the mud.

Cheers erupted from the bank as Clem's legs buckled beneath her and she sank up to her waist in mud. Her eyes met Nick's relieved grey ones as she took the hand he held out and allowed him to pull her to her feet. 'Good job, Red.'

Hand in muddy hand, they made their way to the edge of the bank. Nick looked at the calf and his eyes widened. 'Oh, damn, it's about to collapse.'

He dropped her hand and rushed over to the calf whose knees had buckled beneath it. Jabu and another ranger rushed down the bank to kneel beside him. Nick ran his hands over the calf, shaking his head. 'Dehydrated, weak. We have about an hour to get some fluids into it or we're going to lose it.'

'Andy, get the tarp. Clem, grab a bottle of water from the car and bring it here,' Nick ordered.

Clem scrambled up the bank and caught the bottle of water

Mdu, camera still on his shoulder, threw at her. She ran back to Nick and handed him the bottle. Nick shoved the water into the calf's mouth as Andy returned with the tarp. He opened the tarpaulin and laid it next to the calf. 'We'll roll it on,' Nick instructed. 'Clem, support its head.'

Clem put her hands on either side of the rhino's head as the men rolled its body onto the tarp and helped them push it so that the calf lay in the middle of the heavy fabric.

'Any sign of the mother, Bayanda?' Nick called up the bank.

'Nothing so far, but I'm keeping watch.'

'We're bringing it up, so if she decides to charge, this would be the time,' Nick shouted back and turned back to the group kneeling in the mud. 'We'll each grab a corner. Clem, it'll be tough but I need you. Whatever you do, do not drop your corner, OK?'

Clem nodded. Her arms were weak and shaky with fatigue but they still had to get this animal up the bank, into the vehicle and back to the rehabilitation centre if it had any chance. She couldn't cop out now—she wouldn't. They were relying on her; they needed her. It was a heady, powerful feeling and she felt strength flood her system.

She could do this—she would do this. She grabbed her corner and, with Nick leading the way, carried the little rhino up the bank and lifted it into the back of Jabu's Land Cruiser.

Nick, sitting on the edge of the truck bed, held out his hand to Clem. It felt so natural to step up to him, to rest her head on his upper arm as she tried to get her breath back. Nick dropped a quick kiss on her mud-splattered head. 'Jabs, take Bayanda to the clinic and then can you take Clem home? Andy, you drive me and the calf to the rehab centre...' He looked around when Clem let out a horrified gasp. 'What's the matter, Clem?'

Clem's heart dropped to her toes as she slapped her hand to her chest, realizing that her locket was gone. She bit her lip and looked around wildly before lifting miserable eyes to look into Nick's worried face. 'My mum's locket. It's gone. The chain must've snapped when we were in the mud.' Clem tried to sound brave but she knew her voice was tinged with sorrow as she blinked back tears. 'Sorry, it's not what's important right now. Get the calf back to the rehab centre.'

Nick rubbed his already filthy face with a filthier hand. 'Sorry, Clem. I'll see you back at the house later, OK?'

'Yeah.'

Clem looked at the churned up mud as she made her way to the game viewing vehicle, thinking that somewhere in all that dirt and muck was something she greatly treasured. She nearly asked Jabu to wait while she looked for it but then she heard Bayanda's racking cough, clocked his shaking hands on the rifle he still held at his shoulder, his eyes scanning the bush. He needed to get to the clinic... Maybe she could talk Nick into coming back here later and having a look around.

Oh, it just broke her heart to think it might be gone for ever.

For the second time, Clem stood on the lawn outside Nick's house as Jabu sprayed the worst of the mud from her arms, legs and clothes. He didn't need to know that she had, at the very least, a truckload down her pants and in her bra.

'Do you have to film this?' She glared at Mdu, who just smiled and didn't lower his camera.

'So, how important was that locket to you?' Jabu asked as water pounded off her thighs and mud ran into the grass.

'It was my great-grandmother's and passed down from mother to daughter on my mum's side. It was her favourite piece of jewellery, apart from her engagement ring,' Clem answered, her voice wobbly. 'My mum died in a car accident; I was with her. She was wearing it when she died and I woke up in hospital with it around my neck.'

'So, pretty important, then?'

'Yeah, pretty important,' Clem answered, taking the pipe

from Jabu's hand and putting the nozzle down the front of her shirt. She looked at Jabu and gnawed the inside of her lip.

'Mdu, have you got enough footage of me hosing off?'

'Yep.'

'Then can you excuse us?'

Mdu nodded, closed the camera and walked into the house.

'Jabu, can you tell me about Nick's ex-wife?'

Jabu sent her a strange look. 'His widow,' he corrected and, seeing her confused face, explained, 'Nick is a widower, not divorced.'

'Oh.' Wow. That was unexpected.

'Why would you think that he was divorced?' Jabu asked, curious.

'Dunno.' Clem ducked her head, confused herself. She was sure that Nick had implied that they were divorced… No, he'd said that he was the third wheel in his marriage and she'd just assumed. 'Can you tell me a bit about her?'

'Terra? Practical, cool, calm. I've seen her face down a charging lion with nothing more than a rifle between her and the animal, catch and release a spitting cobra, get her vehicle through flood-swollen rivers. She was tough, resourceful, knowledgeable and she loved the bush.'

Clem's heart clenched. 'Perfect for Nick, then.'

'Mmm.'

'How did she die?'

'Brain aneurism. She complained of a headache and the next morning she was gone.' Jabu shook his head. 'I don't feel comfortable discussing this with you, Clem, however much I like you and think you're great for Nick.'

'But I'm not…cool, practical, knowledgeable,' Clem protested. 'I'm useless at this bush stuff.'

'You are…but…' Jabu shook his head and lifted his hand. 'Let me say this. Working this land has been Nick's greatest passion since he was a boy…sometimes, unhealthily in my opinion, to the exclusion of so much else.'

'A wife, a family...'

'But that was his choice. He shouldn't be alone so much and I think that having you move into his house and his life is the best thing that's ever happened to him.'

'He's taught me so much...about myself.'

'Trust me, you're teaching him stuff, too.'

'Like what?'

'How scary it is to feel again.' Jabu lifted his hand. 'Seriously now, subject closed. So, am I also going to get a preview of your lingerie like Nick did?'

'Is there anything he doesn't tell you?' Clem demanded.

'Not much, no. So am I?' Jabu's dark eyes danced and Clem had to smile, knowing he was teasing.

'No. You're married with three stunning kids and I like your wife.'

'I like her too,' Jabu agreed and rolled his eyes. 'OK, keep your clothes on, then.'

'I intend to.' Clem pushed her wet hair back from her face. 'Do you think the calf will make it?'

Jabu shrugged. 'Fifty-fifty. Nick will do everything for it a vet would do and it's just a matter of time.' He glanced at his watch. 'I've got to get back. You OK here on your own?' he asked before shouting for Mdu, who ambled out of the house, an apple in his hand.

'Sure.' Clem stood in her wet clothes and waved him off as a monkey scampered across the lawn. When Jabu's car was out of sight, Clem shrugged off her wet clothes and walked into Nick's house in her underwear.

This was, she thought, becoming a bit of a habit.

It was mid-afternoon when a clean Clem heard the sound of vehicles outside the door. Pushing away her books—she still couldn't identify the different antelope types except for the ever common impala—she walked to lean against the back door as Nick's battered Landy and the other game viewing vehicle pulled up, each filled with very muddy rangers. And Liam, who looked a great deal cleaner than the others. They all had very broad smiles on their faces and greeted her with whoops and hollers.

'Afternoon, boys,' she said, stepping onto the grass. 'Been wallowing in the mud pool then?'

Nick stepped out of his vehicle and looked at his rangers with pride. 'When the guys heard what you did to save the calf—'

'She's OK?' Clem demanded.

'Yeah, she'll pull through. She'll have to have a full-time nurse and feeder for a while but she'll be fine.'

Clem shot him a broad smile. 'Oh, that's fabulous news.'

Nick walked around his car and leaned against the bonnet. 'As I was saying, the boys heard about your effort to get her out and, on hearing that I was going back to the pan to look for something, they volunteered their services as well.'

'I have no idea what you're talking—'

The words dried on Clem's tongue as she saw the chain wrapped around Nick's hand, the locket dangling beneath his fist. Tears welled, fell and ran down her cheeks. 'Oh, God, that's... You went back to look for it?'

'Mmm.' Nick held it out to her. 'I washed the mud off but the photos inside are ruined.'

Clem gulped as her fingers grabbed the locket. 'I can get copies. Nick, I—'

'Jabu said it was important to you,' Nick said gruffly. 'Andy found it.'

'But it was your idea.' Clem walked into Nick's arms and, not caring that she was getting muddy all over again, buried her face in his neck. 'Thank you so much.'

'Thank you for your help,' Nick said in her ear. 'I couldn't have done it without you. Proud of you, Red.'

More tears rolled and Clem's smile wobbled. Knowing that if she stayed within those strong arms she'd dissolve into a wet puddle at his feet, she backed away and hopped onto the running board of the Landy, leaning forward to kiss Andy. 'I owe you big.'

She leaned in for a hug and got half his mud on her as well.

'You do,' Andy agreed and his white teeth flashed in his filthy face. 'But we all agreed that you could thank us by having Nick hose you down and then stripping down to your underwear.'

'Does anyone not know that I did that?' she demanded, hands on her hips, lips twitching.

Nick banded his arm around her waist and he swung her off the Landy. 'Nope. Boys can't help bragging when they get a free lingerie show from a supermodel.'

'I was never a supermodel and am now ten years older than when I modelled professionally,' Clem protested. 'And no, as grateful as I am, that's not going to happen.'

The rangers groaned theatrically and Clem grinned.

Andy leaned his forearms on the steering wheel and he looked at her, his face now serious. 'You did a good thing today, Red.'

She felt Nick's arm tighten around her waist in agreement, felt the kiss he dropped into her hair. Pride at being a part of accomplishing something that mattered, something that had an impact, rushed, hot and fast, through her.

She still didn't know what the rest of her life looked like but she did know that whatever she did in the future, it would have *meaning.*

CHAPTER EIGHT

Luella Dawson's blog:

> *Did we ever think we would see Clem up to her ears in mud? And how thrilling was that rhino rescue—every animal counts so donate at www.baobab&buffalofoundation.com—and how romantic was the find the locket in the mud scenario?*
>
> *In contrast, Cai and Kiki are boring, self-absorbed, narcissistic and annoying.*
>
> *But the real question and what we all want to know is: what happens when the lights go off at Two-B? Huh?*

IT WAS a full moon and for the past eighty years these special lunar nights were celebrated at Two-B with a picnic on Arthur's Hill, where the guests could watch the moon rise and shine across the river below.

The Full Moon picnic at Two-B was now, to quote the website, an 'experience to delight all the senses'. Tables would be draped in soft, relentlessly bleached cotton cloths, glasses polished, small bouquets of flowers arranged, comfortable chairs would be placed in the best viewing points, a fire would be built in the concrete pit that Nick's great-grandfather had built with his own hands. There would be imported cheeses, battered prawns, snack platters and sushi. French champagne.

The guests, dressed in their most formal clothes, would be greeted with an *Out of Africa* experience, complete with superb views, amazing food and elegantly dressed companions.

It was Nick's greatest wish to experience just one full moon on his own, or maybe with just Clem for company. Instead, he had to play the society host, to guests whose company he didn't particularly always care for but whose money kept the wheels of Two-B turning.

Ducking into the foyer of the Lodge, he skirted the stairs and stumbled into Clem's slim back. Instinctively, his hands shot out to steady her and he found himself gripping a soft, silky rose print dress and could feel softer, fragrant female flesh beneath it.

Nick held her waist but stepped back to take in the low neckline that revealed a lot of her creamy, slightly freckled chest and the edge of a shell-pink bra. Ruffles around the hemline pulled his attention to her gorgeous knees, legs and delicate feet in high, strappy heels.

His intern game ranger, who'd spent the morning mucking out the monkey enclosures at the rehab centre, was gone and Princess Red looked amazing, as if she'd just floated down the stairs from a suite above.

She confused him, Clem thought, not unhappy with the realization. There was nothing wrong, in her humble opinion, in keeping a man off balance. It did make life so much more interesting. And what a man, in his tailored soft black trousers that made his legs seem even longer and more powerful. His light cotton sweater, the colour of soft, newly churned butter, hugged his chest before falling in a straight line to just beneath the waist of his trousers.

'Interesting combination,' Clem said lightly.

Nick glanced down to where she pointed and grinned at his trousers, tucked into black wellington boots. 'Glad you like my sartorial style.'

'Um…no. Why are you spoiling that nice outfit with such revolting footwear?'

'When I was twelve I stepped on a puff adder while watching the moon rise at Arthur's Hill.' Nick shrugged. 'I was lucky, I didn't get tagged but since then…it's my equivalent to your fear of storms.'

Nick steered Clem to the open foyer door and down the front steps to where the guests were arranging their very expensively, sometimes elegantly clad selves and their cameras onto the pew seats of the long wheel base game viewing vehicles.

'Clem and I will take my Landy,' Nick told Andy.

As one, Nick and Clem angled left towards his Landy. Seeing the large wide eyes of a bushbaby peeking out from the branches of a Mopane tree, they stopped to watch the curious animal for a minute.

'It's so cute.' Clem stopped again, this time looking down. She suddenly bent her legs, tucked her dress behind her knees and, crouching in her heels, watched a dung beetle roll an enormous ball of elephant dung across the road.

She made him notice the little things, Nick thought, watching her profile. While the guests were, in general, focused on seeing the predators and the big mammals, Clem was fascinated by everything. While she still couldn't recognize a red hartebeest with a gun to her head, she was fascinated by the birds and the flowers, the history and the culture of the people of the region.

Through her eyes, he was rediscovering his land and his people. Clem stood up and stepped over the dung beetle and, when they reached the vehicle, she headed for the passenger side and glared at the broken door. 'This car drives me nuts! I can't get in in this dress and if I do I'll rip it on the spring.'

Nick started to climb in behind the wheel, stopped and looked at her. 'Then do you want to drive? Do you drive?'

'Of course I drive!' Clem walked around to the driver's door and Nick waited and opened the door and helped her up.

He rested his elbow on the ridge of his half-door as she drove off. 'Another full moon, another moonlight picnic.'

'It's a great idea. How did it start?'

'My great-grandfather—Arthur—was a bit of a pagan and used to come up here to dance naked. He was, apparently, quite eccentric. But so was my great-great-grandfather. Do you know that he used to go on safari with his own feather bed, copious amounts of Burgundy, but no spare ammunition or underwear?'

'Are you being serious?'

Nick grinned. 'Mmm. Rumour has it that he'd also insist that his mistress accompany him and my great-grandmother would love it because he'd always come home with malaria or dysentery or something ghastly.'

'That generation seemed to be a lot more tolerant than us.'

'You seemed pretty tolerant with Campbell,' Nick commented.

'Cai wasn't stupid and he played me like a master. Right at the beginning he warned me that there would always be rumours of him cheating and that it came with the territory. I was young and stupid and, moreover, I wanted to believe him.'

The dark night encouraged conversation and confidences, Nick thought. 'Did you mean what you said about being over him?'

'Yes. I was over him before that stupid interview.'

'But I heard you crying...'

'Not over him.' Nick had to smile at the tart note he heard in her voice. 'I was humiliated and scared and angry that he'd deceived me about having children. And I'd arrived in the middle of nowhere, living in a house with a man who didn't like me and really didn't want me there.'

Fair comment. 'So, if you're so over him, what's your hesitation about me...this heat we have?'

'Let me count the reasons.' Clem's sigh drifted over him. 'Because he was my first and only lover, so I'm a bit naïve about how to handle brief affairs. Because we are living and working together, because I'm leaving…and because I'm still working through why I hooked up with him in the first place.'

Huh. All good and valid reasons. 'Any progress on the last point?'

'Sort of. I think I was looking for love in all the wrong places and for all the wrong reasons,' Clem admitted. 'Does that sound strange to you?'

'No, I understand exactly what you mean.'

Hadn't he done the same thing with Terra? After a lifetime of being the peacemaker in his family, the stable influence, the port in a storm for his volatile family members, he'd vowed he'd avoid drama in his own personal life. He'd been attracted to Terra because she was quiet and self reliant and unemotional. Being young and selfish—and so busy and involved with the establishment of the Lodge—he hadn't realized that even she needed companionship and care and when he did, in the worst way possible, it had been too late.

After he'd erupted and spewed all over his family the week after her funeral, he'd realized that his introverted, loner tendencies caused pain…to himself and to other people.

Ergo, it was better not to get involved.

They reached a fork in the road and Nick indicated that she should veer left. He looked up at Clem's gasp of astonishment as she approached the other stationary vehicles parked off the road. The sun had set, the trees and shrubs were violet silhouettes and the river was a glistening snake in the valley below.

'I've never seen anything like the African night sky. It's like someone opened a packet of diamonds and tossed them like glitter across black velvet,' Clem said, her voice reverent.

It did. It looked exactly like that, Nick thought. He'd grown up with this sky, had mostly ignored it and he'd forgotten how to appreciate it. Looking at it through Clem's eyes, he felt slightly ashamed that he'd forgotten how to look.

'You are so lucky to live here,' Clem said as her hand reached out for his.

As he held her hand, the stars disappeared as the moon started to rise and he knew that she was right. He was lucky. And he realized that while he'd been protecting and caring for his land, he'd forgotten how to love it.

Strange that it took a society princess and city girl to remind him of that.

Clem stood in front of the full length mirror in Nick's bedroom—the only one in the entire house—and stared at herself in the mirror, the zip of the black couture gown three quarters up her side.

It would not go any further and she was about to pass out from the lack of oxygen in her lungs. This could not, in any universe, be happening. She'd been the same size for the past fifteen years... She didn't pick up weight. Ever.

Mdu, very wisely, kept quiet and kept filming. Clem looked at the gold and the pale pink designer gowns which Jason had couriered to Two-B's depot in Mbombela and Jabu had picked up and brought back on the plane that afternoon. They frothed across Nick's king size bed, mocking her.

She didn't fit into either of them any more.

Oh, damn it.

Clem picked up the dress and held it midway up her calves and walked, barefoot, through to the lounge, where Nick was stretched out on the couch watching Sky Sports. He flicked his glance over her and sent her a smile. 'Cool dress.'

Clem put her hand on her hips. 'Well, it would be if I wasn't too fat for it.'

Nick sat up and put his beer on the coffee table. He muted the sound on the TV and spun his index finger in a gesture for her to turn around. Clem obliged him and his mouth twitched when she faced him again.

'Aren't you going to say anything?' she demanded.

Nick shook his head. 'I learnt a long time ago that whatever I say in these sort of "Have I put on weight?" or "Am I fat?" situations will come back and bite me.'

'Good policy,' Mdu said from the kitchen counter, camera on his shoulder.

Clem laughed. 'Well, it's not like the women's sumo wrestling team want to recruit me yet.' She wrinkled her nose. 'What am I going to wear to the ball next weekend? I suppose I could go on a fruit and water diet—'

'Don't you dare. Are you sure the zip isn't stuck?' Nick asked her as he stood up. He stood behind her and Clem felt his fingers on her back. She sucked in a breath as Nick, out of the camera's view, trailed his index finger down the knobs of her spine before grabbing the zip. 'If the ball is next weekend, then that explains why Jessica has been driving me nuts.'

'Who is Jessica?'

'My younger sister. Her marketing company has the contract to do Two-B's marketing, PR and events. The ball is her baby.' Nick tugged the zip and tugged again. 'Uh…Red? This isn't going up.'

'I know; I tried.' Clem bit her lip. 'I'm going to have to get to a city, to try and find an off the rack dress that fits.'

'You're taking this very calmly,' Nick told her, surprised.

Clem's eyes laughed at him. 'Were you expecting me to act like a diva because I picked up some weight?'

'Uh…' Nick hedged, confused at her reaction. Where was the spoilt princess, the society girl? Who was this down-to-earth woman and what had she done with Princess Red? Never would he have thought that Clem would be blasé about the dresses not fitting or the weight she'd picked up.

Oh no, that couldn't be pride he was feeling, could it? He didn't do pride or affection for women any more.

Nick cursed silently. He had to pull away from her, he *had* to get some perspective.

Clem scratched her forehead. 'Maybe Jason could get onto some designers in Johannesburg and see if they can dress me.'

'I'll call Jess and ask her.'

The words were out of Nick's mouth before he could yank them back. He'd kept his relationship with his sister as professional as he possibly could these last couple of years and, by asking for her non-business help, he was cracking that family door wide open again.

'Your sister? How could she help?'

'Jess has all the designers on speed dial. She'll make a plan.'

Clem cocked her head. 'Would you mind doing that for me?'

He didn't have a damned choice now that he'd uttered the words. How could he spin this to Jess to make it sound like a business deal, to keep her curiosity down and his emotional distance intact? It wasn't going to be easy...

Nick looked at his watch. 'I'll call her in the morning. I want to work out, then we're going up to the Lodge for the wine tasting evening, remember?'

Clem wrinkled her nose as she gathered up the gold gown. 'I forgot,' she said, heading for her room. She tossed him a naughty smile over her shoulder. 'I don't drink but, now that I'm fat, I have an excuse to Hoover up Chef's yummy hors d'oeuvres.'

Nick snapped a full round house kick at the punchbag and followed the kick with an upper-cut when the bag came roaring back towards him.

Sweat snaked down his bare spine into the back of his shorts and his hair was matted to his head. Using the back of his wrist, he pushed the hair back from his face and hauled air into his lungs. Usually a good workout cleared his head but all the hour-long assault on his body had left him with was a dull headache and a tall thirst. Pulling off one glove with his teeth, then ridding himself of the other, he reached into the small fridge that stood in the corner of his gym and picked up a bottle of water. Snapping it open, he took a long sip before sinking to sit on an exercise mat.

He'd thought the other night that Clem was his fork in the road but he hadn't realized how big a detour she was turning out to be.

She made him laugh, she made him think and just when he thought he knew how she was going to react then she did a three-sixty on him and blew all his perceptions out of the water. He'd thought she was going to go all diva on him about picking up a little weight—weight that she needed—yet she'd laughed at herself and shrugged it off. Every day she was losing more and more of the princess and the fake society girl and he was enjoying having her around.

Which was, he admitted, not good.

After Terra, he'd become good at being lonely, had welcomed the freedom of not being emotionally involved and the knowledge that he wouldn't be left again, twisting in the wind. In a week he'd gone from being part of a couple, part of a dream to being disappointed, disillusioned and distraught.

He'd vowed never to be put in that position again and yet this sprite of a woman was making him think, and laugh and—he cursed—feel again.

As the glossy veneer of the glamour girl, rock star wife rubbed off, he found himself more and more drawn to this Clem, who cried on getting her mum's locket back, the one who was equally determined—perhaps more so—to save that rhino calf than him, the one who could spend hours on his deck looking at the stars.

The funny, sweet, sarcastic woman who didn't mind leopard cubs nibbling at the diamond studs in her ears at the rehab centre, who still couldn't tell the difference between an eagle and a vulture, who made ugly hiking boots look like a million dollars.

It wasn't supposed to be like this, he thought, resting his bottle against his hot forehead. He'd thought he could dismiss her but her mind was sharper than she realized, her heart was bigger and her stubbornness was legendary. She didn't give up and she didn't give in.

And she was turning out to be more important to him than he'd ever imagined. And that confused and scared the hell out of him. Because he couldn't see any type of future for them.

Anyway, he was still convinced that he was her rebound fling, a stepping stone for her to use to get back into the dating game. And, because she'd been in a serious relationship for so long, surely she'd want to play the field...see who and what else was out there?

Wasn't that what he'd done when he'd come out the other side of what had turned out to be a train wreck of a marriage?

The thought of Clem doing the same made his stomach churn.

Nick heard soft footsteps outside and his heart accelerated. Ignoring her, he remained seated and looked up when she reached the edge of the mat.

'Nick?'

'Mmm?'

'Jabu just radioed, he said that he and Andy are taking Carol on a game drive and do we want to go with them?' Clem replied, her toes curling on the edge of the exercise mat.

Nick stood and whipped the radio out of her hand. '*Mfo*, pick us up in half an hour.'

'Roger,' Jabu replied and Nick tossed the radio onto the exercise mat and looked beyond her and out of the open door.

'And the wine tasting?'

'We can be late,' Nick said. 'Mdu gone?'

'Yeah—aaah.'

Nick clasped her face in his hands, his thumbs rubbing

the arch of her cheekbones. He watched her eyes deepen and when she touched her bottom lip with the tip of her tongue, he swooped.

He knew how to do this, how to give and take pleasure. While he didn't understand a damn thing about the emotions she churned up inside him, he could and did understand this.

A man, a woman, heat and attraction...it had driven human survival throughout the millenniums. He slanted his lips over hers and was swept away by her sweetness, her honest response. Her small hands curled into his hair and her breasts brushed his chest. Her mouth was sweeter and hotter than he remembered, her body more pliant, her response more fervent.

Bad move. Nick mentally slapped himself around the head. How was he supposed to leave it at this, step away when his heart and mind—and other parts of him—demanded more?

He could feel the feminine strength in the arms that hooked around his neck, in the hands that tugged at his hair. He suspected—knew—that there was more of that strength inside her, emotional not physical.

At the last moment, Nick pulled back from seducing her and from the low purr that vibrated in her throat he knew that she wanted him to... No, that she needed him to.

Nick rested his forehead on hers and looked down at her with his amazing eyes. 'What the hell are we going to do about this, Red?'

Clem buried her face in his neck and didn't answer him. She couldn't let him see how much his kisses rocked her, how close she was to giving herself, to begging him to take her. It would give him too much power, too much control... She couldn't let him know that it took everything she had to pretend to be casual about her physical attraction to him

'I...you just touch me and I lose control. It's never been... I've never...' Clem mentally shook her head. Oh well, if she was going to say stupid things like that, then why was she bothering to try and act casual? She might as well lie on the floor and pant like a dog.

Where did these words come from?

'I know. Me too.' Nick rested his chin on her head. If it was just sex then it would be easy, she thought. She might not have had many lovers—OK, one—but she did know that sex was easy; it was the rest of the emotional baggage that came with it that made it complicated.

'I need to shower,' Nick murmured without letting her go.

'Mmm.' Clem disengaged herself from his arms and backed away She rocked on her heels and looked at the ceiling. She wasn't going to ask, she really wasn't...but she did anyway.

'Is Carol that tall blonde I saw walking into the staff canteen earlier? Here to interview for the senior game ranger position? Blue eyes? Big bum?'

Clem winced at the note of jealousy she heard in her own voice.

Cool and sophisticated she wasn't.

'I thought she had a very nice bum,' Nick commented.

Three seconds later, Nick found himself on the exercise mat and Clem grinned at his surprise that she'd swept his feet out from under him.

He leaned back on his elbows and frowned up at her. 'Uh— how?'

'Judo classes.' Clem held out a hand to haul him up. Her mouth curved as he stood up, and she dropped a gentle kiss before speaking against his mouth.

'Remember that the next time you look at her bum. And take a shower, Sherwood. May I suggest a cold one?'

CHAPTER NINE

Luella Dawson's blog:

Anyone who can't see the sexual tension between Clem and Nick on The Crazy Cs must be deaf, blind or just plain stupid—I keep expecting someone to whip out a fire extinguisher to cool them down every now and again.

THE next evening, on hearing that Nick and Clem had nothing more exciting planned than an early night, Liam and Mdu decided to join the rangers at The Pit for their weekly game of poker. Nick watched them leave and shook his head.

'They'll be skinned alive. Those boys are sharks. I'm a pretty good player but Andy nearly cost me my shirt...I bought him beers for about a month.'

Clem placed her elbows on the kitchen counter, her face in her hands. 'I'm starving.'

'You're always starving,' Nick complained. 'For someone so skinny you sure do pack it away.'

'Huge metabolism. But if I don't watch what I'm eating then I won't fit into any of the dresses Jessica has organized for me to wear to the ball. I spoke to her today...Thanks for calling her, by the way.'

Nick shrugged, opened the fridge and peered inside. 'No

problem. Do you want to go to the staff canteen for supper or do you fancy steak, baked potato and a salad?'

'If I don't have to cook it, then I'd love that.'

'Like I'd trust you with a steak,' Nick scoffed.

Clem picked up her mobile and flipped it up and over. 'I had quite a conversation with your sister.'

Nick sent her a quick searching look. 'Really?'

'I felt like a grilled cheese sandwich at the end of the conversation. How are you? Are you seeing someone? Why am I staying with you? Are you happy? Which makes me wonder... when did you last have a proper conversation with her, Nick?'

'We talk about Two-B, the ball,' Nick replied in a tight voice. 'A thousand people, top venue, two bands, gourmet food, fine wine et cetera, et cetera.'

'Did you know that she was mugged three months ago? That she's broken up with her boyfriend? That she's thinking of moving to Cape Town?'

Nick sent her a distressed look. 'Was she hurt?'

'Bumps, bruises. Why didn't you know about that, Nick?'

Nick stared out of the window before turning back to her. Clem thought that his eyes looked haunted.

'Is she sorting out something for you to wear?' he asked in that voice that did not encourage her to pursue the topic on the table. Clem decided to err on the side of caution—for now—and sidestep the subject.

'Well, the designers are sending their gowns, size zero to size two—' Clem pulled a face '—to the hotel suite she's booked for you—us—together with shoes and accessories.'

Clem tested the waters again, using her most neutral voice. 'Tell me about the rest of your family. You have three brothers?'

Nick turned to the fridge and pulled out ingredients for a salad and pushed them towards her. 'Make the salad, Red. You can make a salad, can't you?'

Clem rolled her eyes as she pulled a knife from the cutlery block and proceeded to slice carrots.

'So…your family?'

Nick narrowed his eyes at her. 'One older, two younger brothers, doctor, psychiatrist, teacher. Jess.'

'And your parents?'

'My father is an artist—sculpture and huge oils—and my mother is a university lecturer—English Lit. Mad as fruit bats, both of them.' Nick put the potatoes into the oven and watched her make the salad. 'Growing up, our house was always filled with people. Lots of wine and lots of music. Lots of noise. Now it's just the same, with the addition of my brother's kids. Chaotic. Messy. Complicated.'

'Did they like your wife?' Clem asked, slicing up cucumber. She stared down at the board and wondered why she was pursuing this subject. Why did she need to know about Nick's past, his relationship with his wife? Who was this man who'd been married and widowed and now shut himself off from his family, who so obviously loved and worried about him?

And why?

Nick stole a piece of carrot and nibbled on it thoughtfully. 'I think it was more a case of Terra taking her cue from me and she was only able to cope with them in small doses.'

'I didn't realize she died. I thought you were divorced.' Clem flicked at his fingers but Nick still managed to snag a piece of cucumber.

A curtain fell in Nick's eyes. 'Yeah. Brain aneurism.'

Clem shrugged. 'I heard that she was an amazing wife for someone like you to have. She knew the bush, loved the life.'

Nick stood up and walked to the fridge and pulled out a beer. 'I thought she did but I…it wasn't enough. Juice? Soda?'

'Nothing, thanks. What wasn't enough?'

'All of it.' Nick rolled his beer bottle in his hands. Why wasn't he putting a lid on this conversation, shutting her down to stop her from prying into his past—a past that had nothing to do with his present life or, frankly, with her?

'Talk to me, Nick.' Clem smiled ruefully. 'I won't judge. After all, nobody has had a relationship quite as messed up as mine.'

He had to admit that she had a point. She'd taken stupid relationships to an art form with Campbell but he suspected that the root of all her insecurities was in her relationship with her parents. Campbell was the result, not the cause.

And maybe if he told her his sob story then she'd be sensible and get that he was a complete waste of emotional energy and back away from whatever they had brewing.

He could only hope.

Nick leaned against the counter and looked out of the window. 'We met at uni, we were both studying Zoology. She grew up on game farms and in the bush and said she loved the life. We planned all this together—everything. The Lodge, the rehab centre, the reserve.'

Clem winced. 'So, why didn't it work?'

Nick shrugged. 'She battled with the loneliness, the isolation. The eighteen hour days I spent working, the other six I spent sleeping. Living in a shack while I spent millions on the Lodge. I wasn't paying her enough attention. She wanted to move off the reserve, she wanted friends, a life. I loved the reality of the dream; she hated it.'

'You said you were the third wheel in your marriage. Why?' Clem asked.

'She had an affair. Oh, she said it wasn't but I know differently. She had this...thing with a guy, on the Internet. She spent hours on-line, chatting. I accused her of having an affair; she denied it. They exchanged these personal e-mails, had cyber sex, photos...I don't know what it was any more.'

'She gave her time and directed her energy and her emotions to a man who wasn't you. I'd call that an affair,' Clem calmly said.

Nick rubbed his jaw. 'How come you get that and Terra didn't?'

'Maybe it's because I had a serial adulterer for a partner.'

'She said she was lonely...that it was all my fault.'

Clem shrugged. 'Were you going to get divorced?'

'We didn't have time to even discuss that. In a week I went from thinking I was reasonably happily married to finding out about the Internet affair to her dying.'

Clem looked horrified. 'Oh, Nick, that's dreadful.'

Nick drained his beer. 'I never told anyone about Internet Guy. Nobody knows that...not even Jabu.'

Clem put her knife down and walked over to him, placing her hands on his pecs and her forehead on his sternum. 'Oh, sweetie.'

Nick's voice was laced with pain when he spoke over her head. 'I had to let the guy know...the one she was talking to. I felt that I had to tell him, face to face. He cried like a child. He loved her so much, far more than I did. He wanted to marry her. She was leaving me—the next week—and I didn't even know.'

'Nick...'

Behind him, Nick's hands clenched the counter tops. 'I wish that we'd talked more, that I'd realized that she was so unhappy. I also wish she'd left me sooner so that she could've been happy for a little while...she deserved to be loved like that.'

'I'm so so sorry that you had to go through all that.' Clem wiped her eyes as she stepped away from him.

Nick turned away to grab another beer out of the fridge. Looking at it, he put it back and reached for a Coke instead. He took a deep sip, allowing the tart and sweet liquid to slide down his throat.

Clem reached for his can, sipped and continued making their salad. 'So, why do I get the idea that your relationship with your family fell apart after that?'

Nick rubbed his hand behind his neck. 'It did. You've got to understand what living with them was like, Clem. I was neutral ground, for everybody. Because I wasn't emotional, I was the referee in sibling to sibling fights, sibling to parent fights...hell, parent to parent fights.'

Clem winced.

'After Terra died, they got this crazy idea that I needed one of them to stay with me, on a rotational basis. Because it's what they would have needed if it had happened to them. I said not a chance in hell, but they didn't listen. They nagged me until I agreed to stay with my folks for a couple of days. My siblings were always there and they nearly killed me.'

He sipped, swallowed, looked for the words. 'My family are incredibly intimate people, they want to know every-thing about you and they didn't give me a moment's peace. I just wanted some quiet to work through that last week with Terra—I couldn't tell them what happened—and I had these people constantly yapping in my ear. I lost it. Thirty years of resentment and anger and I cracked...I hurt them deeply and I can't go back.'

Clem nodded her agreement. 'You can't go back but you can go sideways or up or down. Do you know that it's the an-niversary of my mum's death in a couple of days?'

'No, sorry...'

'Fifteen years ago. I've pretty much been independent since then.' Clem shrugged. 'I'm going off the point as there's absolutely no reason why you should know. My point is this: all I've ever wanted was a family who loved me as much as yours seems to love you. Don't throw it away too easily, Nick. No man is an island and all that.'

'I do pretty OK on my own, Clem. I'm better that way.' Nick put his arm behind his neck and stretched. 'I live a hard life. There aren't many women who can cope with it on an on-going basis, as Terra proved to me. It's unending hard work; it's lonely and it's isolated. It's not for everyone.'

He especially didn't think it was for pampered princesses used to all the luxuries and amenities life had to offer. This, especially, isn't the life for you, Red. She could see the warning in his eyes, Clem realized, as clearly as if he'd spoken the words.

Nick stood up and his hand drifted over her head.

'I'm going to work out while those spuds cook. Want to join me?'

Clem looked horrified. 'No, I think I'll go and lie on the lounger and look at birds.'

Nick grinned. 'You mean you'll nod off.'

'That too. Wake me up for supper.'

A few nights later, Clem walked into Nick's room and, placing a hand on his shoulder, shook him awake. Nick bolted up and grabbed her wrist.

'What? What's the matter? Is it a storm?'

Clem shook her head. 'No, not yet.'

'It can't be time to get up; it's still dark.' Nick yawned.

'It's about two in the morning,' Clem told him. 'I've got something to show you. Come with me.'

'Unless you're offering sex, I want to go back to sleep,' Nick retorted, flopping backwards.

'Get up and come look. Please?' Clem pulled back the mosquito net and smiled at Nick's sulky face as he reached for a pair of shorts.

Thunder rolled and Clem shook her head. 'I heard the storm; that's what woke me up and I needed the loo…just come look.'

Clem took his hand and pulled him out of his room and into hers. She tugged him to the window and, pulling back the curtain, pointed to the huge Mopane tree. 'Male leopard with a baboon carcass halfway up that tree.'

She peered out into the darkness and Nick looked over her

shoulder, his arms sliding around her waist in a movement that was as natural as it was automatic.

The leopard lay on the long, low-lying branch of the tree, his kill between his feet and his head lifted to the feel of the wind in his face. Nick's heart sighed. OK, this was so worth being woken up for.

'My favourite predator. Powerful, graceful, most beautiful of the large cats,' Nick said, his head against hers. 'Elusive and strong. He can pull prey twice his own body weight up into a tree. Isn't he stunning?'

'Oh, he is.'

Nick nodded and tightened his hold on her when lightning forked and sizzled. 'It's OK, Clem. You're safe.'

'It's going to be rough, isn't it?' Clem whispered looking from the leopard to the big clouds illuminated by the occasional flash of lightning.

Nick wouldn't lie to her. 'Yes, it's going to be a cracking electrical storm. Come and watch it with me.'

He felt her flinch. 'I don't think I can.'

'Yes, you can. We'll sit on the deck just outside, I'll hold you, we'll chat and we'll watch the storm. It'll be beautiful.'

'I—'

'Will you try? If you can't do it, I'll come inside with you.' Nick spoke softly, his voice encouraging.

'You promise?'

'Yes, I promise.' Nick dropped his arms and looked for, and found, her icy hand and wrapped it in his. 'It'll be OK, Red. Trust me.'

They shared a lounger on the deck, protected from the elements by the long roof and the canvas panels Nick dropped to keep out the approaching rain and the electricity-charged wind. Clem lay between Nick's legs, her back against his chest, the back of her head resting on his collarbone. His strong arms criss-crossed her body and she felt protected and secure within his embrace.

She still flinched as the lightning flashed around them, winced when thunder boomed, but she had to admit that it was primal and wild and...thrilling. Raindrops smacked the earth like mini-bullets and the wind made the branches of the trees sway. One moment she could barely see her hand in front of her face the darkness was so complete, the next she could read a book when lightning flashed.

Nick felt warm and strong and, against her lower back, she could feel the long, straight evidence of his desire. It wasn't threatening or uncomfortable, it was just there, a statement of his need for her. She was woman enough to enjoy it...and admit she wanted him. She wanted that completion, that feeling of being taken, possessed, invaded. She wanted to feel his hot mouth, his strong hands on those secret places that hadn't been touched for so long.

Since she'd arrived at Two-B he'd done an excellent job of seducing her heart and her brain and he'd lodged himself firmly under her skin. When she was out of his arms, she tried to be practical and reasonable about the effect he had on her but when she touched him, or he touched her, rationality and sense flew out of the window.

She now truly, as a woman—and not as a star-struck girl— understood why women made seemingly stupid decisions in the name of lust and attraction and sex.

Touching Nick, being touched by Nick, suddenly seemed as necessary to her as breathing. Actually, if she had to forgo breathing in order to be loved by him then she'd happily do that as well.

Nick, reading her thoughts, placed his hand on her waist and picked her up and turned her, placing her so that she straddled him. After kissing her, long and deep, he murmured endearments in her ear; hard, shocking—sexy—words that had her breath spiking and her pulse jumping. Then his mouth was everywhere she needed it to be and his hands—clever and competent—were everywhere else.

It wasn't graceful, it wasn't sophisticated, it wasn't even proper sex, Clem thought as she collapsed, her hand still trapped in his shorts, his in her panties.

Nick's hands stroked her bottom before pulling her panties straight. 'Well, that hasn't happened to me since I was sixteen.'

Clem moved up his body, curling into him and putting her face into his neck. 'I want you—'

'But?'

'I...I...'

Nick just patted her back and his voice was even when he spoke. 'Not ready? Scared? Bad timing?'

'All of the above.' Clem slid off him, sat on the edge of the lounger with her back to him. Standing up, she walked to the side table, found the box of matches and lit the paraffin lamp on the table. When she turned back to Nick he was sitting up, his hair dishevelled from running his hands through it.

He held out his hand. 'Come and sit down, Red.'

Clem sat opposite him, cross-legged, and looked down at her hands. 'It's complicated.'

'It always is,' Nick said, his hand resting on her thigh.

'I haven't done many things I'm proud of, Nick. Unlike you, I haven't created something lasting, something that matters—that makes a difference. I've wasted a lot of time on stupid, meaningless...things and activities.'

'OK.'

Clem took a deep breath. 'The one thing I do really well is give all of myself, rush into things and, because I don't like to admit failure, I stay stuck in bad situations.'

'And I'm a bad situation?'

'Not bad, just complicated. We have such great chemistry, but the last time I felt this chemistry I ended up making a—what's that expression you use?—a dumpster fire of my life.' Clem met his serious eyes and dredged up a smile. 'And I'll be out of your life soon…'

Nick looked at her for a long, long moment. She could see the wheels turning in his head. When he eventually spoke, it was what she least expected to hear. 'I agree.'

'Excuse me?'

His eyes looked silver by the light of the lantern. 'It's a really bad idea and I hear you. But I also think the main reason you don't want to sleep with me is the same reason I'm wary of sleeping with you.'

'And what would that be?'

'Because we wouldn't be having sex.'

'I've lost you.'

'We would be making love and there are continents between the two.' Nick rubbed his forehead. 'We could've had sex the day after you arrived if that's all we were after. And I did think about it.'

'I—'

'Sleeping together, intimate, proper sex is crossing a line—I agree with you there. By crossing it, we'd then open up a whole Pandora's box of emotional stuff that neither of us is ready to deal with.'

'I—'

'Sex would just speed things up and would put too much stress on a situation that is already stressed to the hilt.' Nick blew out his cheeks. 'Look, I can recognize sex-for-fun women and you're not the type. Sex means feelings and connections to you and you're still working through that stuff with your ex.'

Clem shook her head. 'I'm not thinking about him at all… I'm thinking about me.'

'And that's just another reason not to do this.' Nick's mouth twisted. 'This, you and me, can't go anywhere—we have different lives on different continents and you're leaving soon, so why complicate it further?'

'But I thought you wanted—'

'Of course I do. I'm a man, for God's sake. But I'm mature enough to walk away from something that might be nice right now and could cause chaos tomorrow.'

Clem placed her hands in her lap. 'So, what do we do now?'

'What do you think we should do?'

'Be friends?' Clem wrinkled her nose. 'Do you think we can?'

'We can try.'

Nick swung his legs off the lounger and gestured her to stand up. He bent his head to gently kiss her lips before speaking against her lips. 'This isn't easy for me, Clem, don't think it's easy.'

'It's late and we have to get up early,' he added softly.

Clem nodded her agreement. 'Then I'll go to bed.'

She didn't want to leave but she forced herself to make the very long walk to her room.

She didn't see Nick blow out the lantern or realize that, in a very rare fit of temper, he slammed his fist into the wall.

Clem woke up the next day and stretched, feeling rested and relaxed and... She giggled as she rested her hand on her lower stomach. It was amazing how a good orgasm could make a girl feel giddy. Even though she and Nick had, in a fit of stupid maturity, agreed that pursuing a physical relationship was a bad move...well, she'd always have the memory of what had happened on the deck.

She started to hum and drifted towards the shower. Nobody had *ever* told her, showed her, how fabulous sex could be and if that was just a taster...*Mamma Mia!*

She stepped into the shower and picked up her soap and, as its fragrance drifted up to her nose, recollections of what day it was slapped her across the face. She stumbled and slumped against the wall. This was the same soap her mother had always used and she'd carried on the tradition.

Her mum had been dead fifteen years today and she'd forgotten, lost in sexual daydreams. She never forgot, never once in all this time, nothing had *ever* distracted her from the importance of the day.

Clem whimpered and rested the side of her head against the shower wall as water slid off her body. The fall from contentment to despair was instant and complete.

She sank to the floor of the shower and, sitting on her haunches, she wrapped her arms around her knees as her tears mingled with the shower water.

She'd forgotten… *How could she?*

Nick, thanks to several contributing factors to his hellish day, knew that his temper was simmering at somewhere just below explosive. Due to a permit snafu, the rhinos at the reserve up north hadn't been moved yet and every day they remained there, unprotected, they were at risk. One of his sous chefs had resigned, which meant a tiresome search for a replacement who would suit Chef's insane standard of perfection and his—less insane—budget.

And the damned VAT return was due. He hadn't even touched the fact that two of his rangers had come to blows in The Pit the night before and that the plane needed to go in for a service.

And he had the sex life of a teenager. Frustrated was too mild a word to describe his state of mind. Irritated, aggravated and annoyed were closer to the mark but still inadequate.

Friends? He replayed last night. *What a joke.* His libido refused to acknowledge his brain and the party continued in his pants.

And his hand was throbbing like a bitch.

Nick settled down at his desk and pulled up his accounting program to run his tax reports and shook his head at the brisk rap on his door. All he needed was a half hour to get this done... Was that asking too much?

Nick lifted his eyebrows at Megan, who half opened his door to look in. 'Yeah, Megs?'

Megan held the door behind her back and shifted from foot to foot. 'Nick, can I ask you a favour?'

'It's not a good time, Megan.'

'Um...the Sheikh, the one from Bahrain, is due to arrive in half an hour and I have a little crisis. Can you meet him and show him to his cottage?'

Nick glanced down at his dirty golf shirt and grubby blood and muck streaked trousers. He'd been up at the animal sanctuary removing a snare from a jackal's leg and he was less than fresh. 'I'm filthy, Megan. What's the crisis?'

'Monkeys have got into cottage number five and have wrecked the place.'

Nick winced. 'Normal destruction or did they go to town?'

'They tossed the place and have urinated everywhere.'

'Damn it. Housekeeping?'

Megan winced. 'We gave them the afternoon off for Mama Bhengu's funeral and the rangers are all in the field. I asked... Look, I need to fix the cottage for the Wilsons and I need to be here so can you help me with one or the other?'

Nick narrowed his eyes. 'You asked Clem, didn't you?'

Megan looked deeply uncomfortable. 'Yeah...she was most...she said that she'd rather eat slugs.'

Nick abruptly stood up and his chair skittered backwards. 'She's been in a mood all day—' they both had, due to too much emotion and too little sleep, but if he had to keep going then so did she '—and I'm sick of it. Where is she?'

Megan shifted from foot to foot. 'She took your Landy back to the house.'

'She what?' Nick roared. 'Without protection? If it broke down or she had an accident—'

'I radioed her; she got back safely.'

'That's not the point! I'm going to kill her!'

Megan grimaced as he stormed past her. 'OK, but first... can you sort out cottage number five?'

It took Nick an hour and a half to fix the cottage, to mop and disinfect the walls and surfaces, to change the linen on the bed and to replace broken lamps and vases.

His mood had climbed from simmering to volcanic and he found himself gripping the steering wheel of a spare vehicle as he made his way home. Sorting out the cottage had been the perfect end to an awful day. He was tired, frustrated and he still had to deal with Clem.

Oh, joy.

Nick pulled up and hopped out of the vehicle, sending a kudu bull behind the thicket opposite the lawn a cursory glance. He flung open the door and stormed into the house, tossing his radio and keys on the dining room table. Liam shot up from his seat in the lounge and hoisted his camera. Nick glared at him as he stalked past.

'If you know what's good for you, you'll keep that thing out of my face. Clem!'

When she didn't answer he walked down the passage and, without bothering to knock, he opened the door to her bedroom. Clem, towel drying her hair, walked out of the bathroom and turned to look at him. Her eyes skittered away and she stared at the floor.

When she spoke, her voice was toneless. 'I'm asking you, as nicely as I can, to just leave me alone. Please?'

'That's not going to happen,' Nick flung back as Liam slinked past him to take up a position in the far corner. Nick noticed that her eyes were red rimmed but, at that particular moment, he didn't care.

'Is this about last night?' he asked.

If he had been a lesser man then her look would have withered him on the spot.

'Then you have exactly five seconds to find a good reason why you couldn't clean that cottage.'

Clem hung the towel over the back of a chair and shrugged. 'I don't have one.'

'Excuse me?'

Clem shrugged. 'I didn't feel like it.'

Nick felt his pulse beating in his head and he bit the inside of his mouth to keep his temper in check. 'You didn't feel like it?'

Clem walked over to the chest of drawers and reached for some body lotion. She placed her foot on a chair and rubbed the lotion up her long legs. 'No.'

Nick felt the stirring in his body and that just added fuel to the fire. 'Clem, I had to sort out the cottage. Megan couldn't and there was nobody else. I have a million things to do...'

'Then go and do them and leave me alone.'

'Is that all you have to say?'

'Sorry,' Clem replied in a voice that was devoid of emotion. It certainly held no apology.

'I thought we'd moved beyond you acting like this.'

'Obviously not.'

Nick shoved his hands into his hair, ignoring the little voice inside him that was insisting that he was missing a great deal of this puzzle. He was too furious to consider why she was acting like the worst version of herself.

Maybe it was time she left. He was mad enough, frustrated enough to think her going was a reasonable solution to his current problem. The words were out of his mouth before he thought them through. 'If I can't rely on you, then call your father and tell him to send the jet.'

He yanked his mobile from his pocket and handed it to her. 'Just dial five.'

Clem looked at the phone as if it was a snake about to bite her, but she eventually took the mobile with a shaking hand and pressed five. Nick stared at her bent head and wondered what the hell he was doing. She wasn't supposed to call his bluff; he didn't want her to leave. He cursed and reached for the mobile but she backed away.

'Dad? I need to come home. Can you come and get me?'

Nick watched as Clem held the phone to her ear, unable to hear Hugh's voice. When he saw her wipe her eyes with the tips of her fingers, he frowned. The sense that there was something bigger happening here than he was aware of started to grow, smothering his anger.

'OK. Yeah, I'll be fine.' Clem's voice cracked and she dropped the hand holding her phone to her side. Her face was blotchy when she lifted it to look properly at Nick. 'My father won't send the jet today. He wants me to call him again in the morning.'

'That's not...I...Clem, what's going on?' Nick demanded, now thoroughly confused.

Clem handed him his mobile, backed away and shook her head. 'I'm asking you, and Liam, to leave me alone. Please? I know I've been every type of bitch today but I'm asking this one last thing of you. Please, just go.'

Nick, not knowing what else to do or say when confronted with such a worn, beaten down Clem, just looked at Liam and jerked his head.

They both did as she asked and Nick walked straight to the deck. He grabbed the railing and stared at the land below him. This was...pure BS, he decided. She wasn't that spoilt girl any more... Something had gone badly wrong since the very early hours of this morning.

He hadn't the faintest clue what but, knowing Clem, anything was possible.

Telling Liam to stay put, he strode back to Clem's room, opened her door and closed it behind him. Clem was sitting on the edge of the bed, her face wet with tears. His anger gone, he crouched on his haunches in front of her and wished he could shove his hand inside her heart and yank out all her pain, literally suck it out of her so that she could be free of whatever was making her cry.

'Talk to me, Clementine.'

Clem hunched her shoulders under her ears and pulled her bottom lip between her teeth. She stared at a point beyond his head. 'I woke up feeling so good...I was cheerful, thinking of you, last night. I was singing. Singing, Nick!'

'Singing's not a crime, Red.' Well, in Campbell's case it was but that wasn't the point right now. Nick placed his hand on her pale, freckled knee and wondered if Campbell had ever held her, understood her, listened to her. Probably not. After all, he hadn't understood or listened to Terra.

Maybe he'd been too busy, or he'd subconsciously decided Terra didn't need or want his comfort, this girl, at this moment, did. He had to—no, he needed to—listen, to dig, to try to understand whatever was going on in that head of hers. Comforting her, protecting her, making life a little easier for her seemed, at the moment, more important than guarding his emotions.

'I forgot that it's the anniversary of my mum's death today.'

Oh, damn.

'I was singing and thinking—' Clem's voice faltered '—about sex.'

'That sounds pretty normal, sweetheart. To think about those things and to forget for a little while. So normal, Red.'

'I'm so far away from her, Nick. For the last fifteen years, I've put pink roses on her grave. No matter what, it was always a priority. But I'm here and I can't.'

'Does it matter so much, Clem?'

He could see the answer in her eyes; it meant a great deal to her...a daughter's tribute.

Well, he couldn't fly her to London; that was obviously impossible. Did it really matter where she went to visit her mum? Graves were graves... In his mind, it was the thought, the idea that counted.

It might not work but he would do what he could.

Nick pulled her to her feet. 'Wash your face and blow your nose. No, don't ask, just trust me, OK?'

Nick pushed her towards the bathroom and, when she was out of earshot, immediately called Megan. 'Megs, my turn to ask a favour. Are there any pink roses on the premises? I don't care if you have to steal them from the arrangements...'

Clem didn't want company but still found herself at the butt end of the world, hot and unhappy, on a game drive she had no interest in. At least Nick wasn't talking; in fact he hadn't said one word since he'd walked back into her room and led her out.

Why couldn't he understand that she just wanted to be left alone? This one day out of three hundred and sixty-five...

Nick pulled to a stop and Clem lifted her head to look around. She could see it was a graveyard surrounded by an old wrought iron fence. An enormous baobab created shade for the area and a wooden bench rested at its base.

Nick reached behind him and picked up a loose bunch of pink roses from behind her seat and handed them to her.

'It's our family graveyard, Clem. I know it's not where your mum is, but the ritual is the same.' Nick ran a gentle hand from her shoulder to her hand. 'Go mourn your mum, Red.'

Clem gripped the roses in her fist. After a long moment, she stepped out of the vehicle and walked to the graveyard and through the rusty gate. Feeling unsure, she walked over to the wooden bench and perched on the edge of the seat. She rested the roses across her lap and looked up into the branches of the baobab tree.

She waited for the despair, the guilt and the soul sucking pain to drop over her but none of them arrived. Instead, Gina's words drifted past and Clem frowned as she reached out to try and clasp the swirling truth within them.

'You are not your mother.'

'It...was her failing and not yours.'

Could Gina possibly be right? Had she been chasing a mental phantom that she had no chance of catching or changing, all these years?

Her mum had been brilliant at so many things but not at being a mother…and maybe that was OK, maybe she could forgive her for that. Her childhood was over and she could either keep feeling resentful or she could accept that her mum had been a flawed human being who had done the best she could.

Just as she had to do the best she could with who and what she was.

Which raised the thought…who was she? If she didn't have to be the daughter she thought her mother would be proud of, the ditsy society girl the press routinely portrayed or a rock star's companion, then who was she?

Clem. You are Clem.

Her thoughts, as they jumped in and out of her head, became crystal clear.

She wasn't afraid of hard work, Clem thought, or of getting her hands dirty. She really sucked at animal identification and she was getting better at being woken up before the sparrow's yawn.

She loved this land—the heat, the animals and the happy people who worked it. If she went back to live in a city it might kill her or, at the very least, stifle her lust for life.

And she loved seeing Nick's face first thing in the morning and last thing at night.

Clem picked her feet up and put her heels on the bench. It was time to show the world, show yourself, she decided, that she could use her heart and her brains to do something that made a difference.

It was time to be Clem.

Clem felt resolve stiffen her spine. It was time to start a new life. And Nick—where in this exciting puzzle of her new life did he fit? She knew that she was three-quarters of the way to being in love with him, and that she could see herself living with him, here on his land. But she knew that she couldn't make him love her, she could only be a person who was worthy of love. He would never leave Two-B and it was up to him to decide whether he wanted her there or not.

And she'd be OK. She had to be OK. But she could protect herself a little better, pull back a bit, keep a lid on the pot of emotional and sexual tension that was bubbling away.

She had to look after herself; if she didn't, nobody else would.

Clem felt the tension seep out of her shoulders and, after wiping her face with her fingertips, she sniffed. She noticed the newest grave, knew that it was Nick's grandfather's. She gently placed the roses on his grave and picked up a stone and placed it on top of his headstone. Taking a minute to just be, she stood there with her head bowed, listening to the breeze dancing through the big tree. Many long minutes later, she walked back to the Landy and sent Nick a tremulous smile.

'Thanks.'

'Yeah.' Nick placed his forearms on the steering wheel and looked at her. 'Normally, I'd pour a huge glass of wine down your throat but, since you don't drink, I figured chocolate was the next best thing. There's a choc nut sundae being prepared at the Lodge with your name on it. Interested?'

Clem dropped her head and stared at her hands. He offered comfort so easily, she thought, innate kindness in a steady, strong, unsentimental way. What a stunningly perfect gesture. Which made him so much more dangerous...

It was a good time to put her theory of distancing herself into practice.

'Thank you, but I won't. I'd like to go back to the house and have a long, long bath, if that's OK with you.'

'No problem.'

She had to say it, had to apologise. 'Sorry if I was a brat today.'

Nick flashed her a quick grin. 'And there's the reason why you are still sitting on a broken seat.'

CHAPTER TEN

HE WAS going to kill them both, Nick decided, pulling into the
driveway of his childhood home in Johannesburg and pressing
the button on the intercom. Clem and Jess were blackmailing
him into dealing with his parents and he didn't appreciate it.

The gates swung open and Nick, from an old habit, long
forgotten, parked his car under the oak tree to the side of the
garage and looked at his old home. Nothing had changed,
he thought; the garden was as wild, there was a new metal
sculpture by the fish pond, his mother's car was still hap-
hazardly parked as close to the flamingo-pink front door as
she could get it.

God, would this day never end? He and Clem had flown in
from Two-B late this morning with minimal conversation and
Jess had met them at the airport and whipped Clem away—
she'd booked appointments for Clem at a spa, followed by a

consultation with a hairdresser and stylist. Jess was supposed to call him and tell him where he could collect Clem and it wasn't supposed to be at his parents' house.

The nosy, interfering witch.

It wasn't as if he didn't have enough on his plate, he thought; he didn't need the stress of dealing with his family issues as well. He had a million things to do back home *and* he had to get through the ball tomorrow night.

Right now he felt that he'd rather be gored by a black rhino.

Nick tipped his head back against the headrest. With Clem's arrival, his calm, ordered world had been turned upside down and inside out; he didn't like it and, worse, he didn't know how to deal with it. She yanked emotions to the surface that he had no clue how to deal with, that he didn't want to deal with.

Terra issues, family issues, love issues...all those *issues* he'd so studiously avoided.

And something was definitely up with Clem. Since yesterday afternoon, after visiting the graveyard, she had been quiet and reticent and introspective. She wasn't sulking— he knew her well enough to know the difference—but he couldn't put his finger on what was wrong. It was as if she'd put up a wall between them and he didn't like it... He was the one who built walls, not her.

He missed her chatter, her questions, her enthusiasm... If he felt like this while she was around, then how would he cope when she left? And it was becoming more and more difficult to contemplate her leaving.

He felt like a spring about to snap.

Why hadn't he shot himself in the foot when he'd first met her? At the time he'd thought it would be less hassle than having her around... Hell, he should've just shot himself in the heart and done it properly.

Clem knocked on the frame of the door and he jumped. He scowled at her and rested his arm on the window.

'Whose idea was this?' he growled.

'Jess needed to pick something up from her mum and I got invited in. Then they invited me, and you, to stay for dinner. If you don't want to go inside, then Jess will run me back to the hotel later.'

Nick pushed his fingers into his hair. 'Why are you doing this, Clem? Whose side are you on?'

Clem sent him a sad smile. 'Yours, Nick. But I really like your sister and I think she might like me. We had such fun today. Your father wants to show me his art and your mum wants me to taste her apple pie—'

'She's a really bad baker,' Nick grumbled.

'And she wants me to tell her whether her gown is suitable for the ball tomorrow night.'

Nick's eyebrows flew up. 'What?'

'They have all bought—parents and brothers and wives— full price tickets for the ball—'

'They can't afford that! What the hell do they think they are doing?' Nick bellowed. 'Are they freaking insane?'

Clem lifted a bare shoulder. 'Maybe they just want to show their support for you and what you do in the only way they could. In the only way you'd let them.'

Ouch. Nick put his forehead on the steering wheel. He cursed. 'Damn it, Red. I'm just not ready to face them yet.'

Clem briefly touched his hair. 'That's fine, Nick. Nobody is holding a gun to your head, least of all them. I'll get Jess to drop me off at the hotel after supper. I won't be too late.'

Nick shook his head. 'There's a pub we used to hang out at down the road. I'll wait there until you're done. Call me and I'll come and pick you up.'

Clem nodded and turned away.

'Clem?' Nick waited until she turned around before he spoke again. 'Tell them that...no, don't worry.'

'What, Nick?'

Nick shook his head and started the car. How did he explain that he missed them, that he was trying to find his way back without sounding like a complete wimp? He caught Clem's soft eyes and small smile and thought that maybe he didn't need to say the words, that she already knew what he was trying to say.

Although the ball was being held in the hotel they were staying in, they did still have to do the red carpet thing, Jess told them, and so Clem found herself being ushered out of the back entrance of the hotel and into a limousine. The driver took her, Nick, Mdu and his camera around the block and pulled up in front of the hotel, where a ten-deep hedge of photographers and paparazzi stood behind a velvet rope, cameras flashing.

It was déjà vu, Clem thought, hearing the roar outside, the incessant flashes of a hundred cameras. Her stomach clenched and she closed her eyes. If her epiphany in the graveyard hadn't been enough, this situation would've made her realize how far she'd travelled recently. Mentally and physically. The thought of cameras in her face, the incessant, demanding questions made her feel ill.

She didn't want to do it; she wasn't that person any more.

Clem sneaked a glance at Nick, looking so gorgeous in his tailored tuxedo. What would he say if she told him that she'd bought her ticket home, that she'd be leaving Africa a week today? Would he be sad? Relieved? Upset?

You have to leave, she told herself. But oh, how she wished he'd ask her to stay.

Head and heart, she thought. The argument raged on.

Nick looked across at Clem when she heaved a huge sigh. 'You OK?' he asked.

Clem shrugged before dredging up a smile. 'I was just wishing I was on your deck watching the kudu buck coming in to drink.'

Nick's mouth twitched. 'Do you mean the water buck or the kudu?'

'Either. Both. What's the difference?'

Nick shook his head. 'Only two different animals.' He looked out of the window. 'But I agree with you. A beer and a sunset…'

The limousine driver opened the passenger door and Mdu climbed out.

Clem looked across at Nick as he started to leave the vehicle. 'Nick?'

The crowd, recognizing him, roared as he looked back at her. 'Don't leave me, OK?' she asked. 'Whatever they ask, just keep smiling or, at the very least, don't give them a reaction. But please don't leave my side.'

Nick nodded. 'You've got it, Red.'

He held out his hand for her and felt the fine tremors buzz through her fingers as her foot met the pavement. The crowd screamed and the cameras flashed as Clem stood next to Nick on the red carpet. Nick, seeing her flash of panic, tucked her icy hand into his and turned his head to speak in her ear. 'You look good, Red, but I still think nothing beats Stinky Clem in scarlet underwear or Muddy Clem or Grumpy-in-the morning Clem.'

Clem flashed him a huge, genuine smile that banished the nerves from her eyes and replaced the fear with laughter. 'Well, I'm going to try and channel Charming Clem.'

'Impossible,' Nick teased. 'No such thing.'

But there was, Nick realized, two minutes later. While nobody knew that her hand was gripping his with the strength of a twenty-foot African Python, she charmed and flirted with the press, posing for the cameras with ease and confidence.

In amongst the barrage of camera flashes, she deflected the shouted questions flung at her head. She answered with non-answers and Nick, deciding that five minutes was more than enough time for them to be bombarded, placed his hand on her back and steered her towards the entrance.

'I need a drink,' he muttered as he approached Jess and the other members of his foundation's board.

'I need a bath,' Clem retorted. 'I'd forgotten how sleazy they are.'

An hour later, Nick looked across the ballroom and saw Clem surrounded by his entire family, laughing at something his father was saying. He wanted to be with her, Nick realized, wanted to be with them. This was his fault, he admitted; he'd created this rift between them and it was up to him to fix it. In another universe, Clem would be his filter to his family; she would be happy to be involved in the chaos and the emotion and would shield him from their drama. She'd create the space for him to enjoy them.

But he and Clem wouldn't be together so he had to find a way to deal with them. But first he had to try and heal what he had broken.

Clem responded to something his brother Patrick said and caught his eye. He saw the encouragement in the slight tilt of her head, the support in her eyes. Nick took a sip of his whisky, placed the glass on the tray of a passing waiter and excused himself from his companion. He walked towards Clem and his family, feeling as if his heart were about to beat out of his chest.

Clem's smile was like a guiding light and he didn't realize that he automatically reached out for her hand when he reached the now silent, wary group.

He kept his eyes on his mother's face—full of loving forgiveness, eyes brimming—and bent down to kiss her cheek. 'Hi, Ma.'

His mum put her hand on his cheek as he tightened his grip on Clem's hand. 'Welcome back, baby.'

Jess walked up to Nick and wrapped her arm around her mother's waist. He'd picked up an entourage, Nick smiled to himself, his parents were now glued to his side and his brothers and their wives floated up and away from them. Strangely, and surprisingly, he was…OK with that. It was almost as if they thought he might vanish again and they weren't prepared to let him out of their sight. Nick placed his hand on his sister's back and looked down at her. 'Problem, Shrimp?'

Jess fiddled with her gold chain and flashed him a mock-irritated look at the use of his old nickname for her.

'I've been trying to keep up with Clem, trying to keep track of the pledges that she's wiggling out of all and sundry and I've lost track.' Jess sighed. 'It's like magic—she smiles at someone and they open their wallet. I'm worried that I haven't captured them all.'

Nick looked across at Clem, her hair a beacon across the room. She looked elegant in a simple yet dazzling floor-length gown of graduated shades of green, the lightest shade echoing her eyes and moving subtly down to the hem, where the green was so dark it almost looked black. She stood, tall and slim, with an easy smile on her face. Her bald companion looked besotted.

Nick could relate, he suspected it was the same expression he often had on his face when he looked at Clem.

He pulled his attention back to Jess. 'I wouldn't worry about it. Beneath the gorgeous face is a razor-sharp brain; she'll remember who she has winkled money out of.'

'She looks fabulous,' Jess sighed. 'And, surprisingly, she's so nice.'

'Yes, she is.' Nick's heart bumped as Clem lifted her eyes to look for him and, when their eyes met, she sent him a barely discernible wink. Jess smoothed his lapels and patted his chest as his mum put her hand on his arm.

'Go dance with her, Nick. You know you want to,' his mum suggested.

'I do.' Nick squeezed her shoulder before making his way across the room. Excusing Clem from the man she was talking to, he steered her to the dance floor and pulled her towards him. Nick bent his head to place firm lips on her temple. His hand rested on her hip and he yanked her closer as the tempo of the music changed from feisty to slow.

His hand curled around hers and his chin briefly rested against the side of her head as he pulled her into his arms and swayed with her to the slow seductive beat.

Clem cocked her head as the heat from his hand on her hip rocketed up her spine. 'I see that your parents haven't left you alone. Do you want me to distract them for you?'

She just understood him, Nick thought. No words, no explanations.

Nick shook his head. 'No, it's fine. Clem...'

'Mmm?'

His words trembled. 'Thank you. I don't know if—'

Clem placed her fingers against his mouth. 'Just seeing you talking to your dad, dancing with your mum, made my evening. And theirs.'

Nick pulled her closer. 'Are you having fun? You look like you are. You're so good at this social stuff.'

'And you'd rather be at Two-B, fixing something.'

'I would, I admit it. I feel like I am suffocating in this tux.'

Clem's fingers played with the hair at his neck. 'You look good in it, though. Nice to see you in something other than khaki shorts.'

'Thanks. You, however, look...spectacular. I should have told you sooner but I was at a loss for words.'

Nick's chin rested against her temple as they moved slowly across the dance floor. Clem couldn't help placing her forehead on his shoulder, rubbing against the softness of his exquisitely cut black suit. Heightened senses, she thought. It was the smell of Nick, spicy and masculine, the feel of him—solid and strong—his heat, the slow beat of the music languidly pulsing the blood in her veins. His hand on her lower back pulled her closer and they were chest to chest, stomach to stomach.

This was ridiculous, she mused, so conscious of the miasma of sensations swirling around them. Lust, attraction, yearning, desire… He was just Nick and this was just a dance.

Except she felt Nick's lips in her hair and felt the power of that brief kiss right down to her toes.

'Clem—this is killing me,' Nick muttered, his voice low and laced with frustration.

Clem's hand clenched on his shoulder. 'I know. I feel the same. I want you so much it hurts.'

Nick groaned and neither of them noticed that they were swaying so slowly that they were practically standing still. Green eyes held grey as emotions tumbled and churned. Clem sucked in her breath and gripped the lapel of Nick's jacket.

'I don't want to not sleep with you tonight. In fact, I don't want to sleep. Let's not sleep, Nick.'

Nick's fingers tightened on her waist. 'What are you saying, Clementine?'

Clem's eyes were clear and direct when they met his. 'Take me to bed, Nicholas. Make me yours.'

'It's not a good idea, Clem. We know this.'

'I'm sick of being sensible and smart. I want to feel and I want you.'

Nick's eyes darkened and they held hers. 'You sure, Red? You don't get to change your mind halfway through.'

'Yes, I'm sure. We've been building up to this for weeks and I don't think I can do another night without knowing what you feel like.'

Nick muttered an oath. 'You kill me, Red.'

For the sake of propriety, Clem pulled back so that there was a hair-sized space between them. 'When can we leave?'

Nick's hand on her back pulled her back to where she was. 'After the auction we can slip out.' He rested the side of his head against Clem's and sighed. 'I want to leave now.'

'Me too. What if I just offer you a million for everything on auction and we get it done?'

Nick's thumb brushed her cheekbone. 'It's a measure of how much I want you that I'm seriously considering that offer.'

CHAPTER ELEVEN

Luella Dawson's blog:

Will somebody please send Clem and Nick a memo? Hire a plane to write it in the sky? Tattoo it across their foreheads? They are so insanely, utterly, besottedly in love with each other that it makes this old cynic—long divorced—want to start believing in the power of love again!

On a related subject...Cai has been very quiet and that makes me nervous. What is the man up to?

THE minor items donated for the auction had been sold off and had received record prices. The free alcohol and convivial atmosphere had loosened wallets and reckless offers were made and accepted by Jess and, beyond her gracious smile, Clem could almost see Jess calculating the proceeds. *Ching-ching,* her eyes shouted when they met Clem's as she passed over gold-covered envelopes to the bid winners, explaining how and where they could collect their purchases.

Clem kissed cheeks, murmured thank yous and endured the occasional squishy hug as Nick looked on, standing below at the front of the audience, flanked by his parents and brothers. Good-looking bunch, Clem thought. She sent him a secret smile when he shot back the cuff on his tuxedo jacket and tapped his watch. She had to drop her head to keep the guests from seeing her flushed cheeks and heavy eyes.

She was going to spend the night with Nick.

The auctioneer started the auction for the last item, a week's stay at the tented camp at Two-B, and the bids flew in thick and fast. Every person there knew that there was a long waiting list and would've paid whatever they could to jump the queue. Eventually, the bids headed past ridiculous and trickled off and three men were fighting for the prize, out-bidding each other in increments of five thousand. After ten minutes, to someone who was eager to get her hands on Nick's hot body, it started to get tedious and she wished someone would just make a huge offer and get the auction over with.

'One hundred and twenty-five thousand...' the auction-eer intoned.

The voice was clear, rude and achingly familiar when it floated across the heads of the guests from the back of the room. 'Oh, for the love of God! This is excruciating! Two hundred thousand... How much is that? Twenty thousand dollars? OK, my bid. Two hundred thousand!'

'Going once, going twice...'

Clem watched in horror as the crowd parted and Cai strode through the buzzing crowd, dressed in a purple velvet tuxedo, his long, streaky blond hair falling out from under a cream fedora. Clem's mouth fell open as she battled to breathe—from what rock had he slid out from under?

'Sold to Mr Cai Campbell,' the auctioneer announced as Cai bounded up onto the stage. She was still taking in his presence when his arms encircled her waist and his soft—yuk!—mouth dropped onto hers. Clem considered raising her knee but she couldn't, not just because her dress didn't allow it but also because she remembered that both Liam's and Mdu's cameras—and the cream of Johannesburg soci-ety—were catching every frame of this disaster movie.

Cai pulled back and Clem narrowed her eyes at him. 'What are you doing here?' she said in a low voice.

Cai didn't bother to moderate his tone. 'I've come to claim my woman.'

'Like hell—' Clem hissed and bit her tongue as Cai stepped away from her, grabbed the stunned auctioneer's microphone and dropped to one knee.

Oh, no, please. Clem closed her eyes. He wasn't going to make some huge romantic gesture, was he?

'Clem, I've been ten different kinds of an idiot.'

You still are, Clem silently told him. Needing support, she reached out and found Jess's hand and held on with a death grip.

'I love you. I have always loved you. You are my sun and my moon and...'

What utter twaddle. Cai had no idea of who she was, what she wanted. To him, she was a pretty face and an acceptable body who had a surname that would always capture the interest of the press.

That was all he needed from her and it wasn't, in any universe, fractionally enough for her.

'...I can't live without you. Please say you'll forgive me, my darling, darling girl. I'll be a better man, I promise you. Will you marry me?'

Clem couldn't help it. A laugh bubbled up from inside her and the more she tried to subdue it the bigger it got. He looked so ridiculous, kneeling there in his purple suit and stupid hat and his ultra-pointy shoes...like the worst caricature she could imagine of an ageing pop star with a Peter Pan complex.

Clem turned to share the joke with Nick and his hard, cold expression made her frown. He had the same look of utter concentration that he had when he was dealing with a major problem or facing down an aggressive animal. She didn't like the fact that his piercing, infuriated gaze stayed fixed on Cai's face.

Clem silently cursed as she felt Jess squeezing her hand. Lifting her eyes, she caught Jess's infinitesimal nod at Cai and her unspoken plea to save the ball she'd worked so hard to make a success.

Right, so this was where she used every acting skill Cai had told her she didn't have.

Looking for and finding her biggest smile, she held out two hands to Cai and when he placed his hands in hers she pulled him to his feet. Reaching to kiss first one cheek and then the other, she muttered in his ear, 'You utter jerk. What do you think you're doing?'

She then took the microphone and placed her hand on her heart. 'Cai, you always did know how to set a party alight. Now, you and I are not going to bore these delightful people with any more of our dramas...'

'We're not bored!' someone yelled and laughter skittered around the room. 'What's your answer, Clem? You going to marry him or what?'

Clem held up her hand. She'd rather eat scorpions. She patted Cai's shoulder with the tips of her fingers. 'Cai has a flair for the dramatic but he knows, as well as I do, that our time has passed. Thank you for the offer, but no, I won't marry him.' She sent the audience a dazzling smile. 'Ladies and gentlemen, thank you for your donations to support the important work Nick and his staff are doing at the Baobab and Buffalo. Jessica?'

Jessica mouthed a thank you as she took the microphone and proceeded to wrap up the evening.

Clem walked across the stage, down the stairs and took the hand Nick held out to her.

'You OK?' he asked her, worried. He pushed his hands into her hair and tipped her face up to look into her eyes.

'What a prat.' Clem shook her head. 'Sorry about that.'

Nick shook his head and dropped his hands from her head.

He muttered an insult that had his mother's eyes widening. 'Nicholas James!'

Nick winced and looked embarrassed. 'Sorry, Mom, but really!'

'Pat and I had to hold Nick back when Campbell kissed you,' Christopher, the brother closest in age to Nick, merrily told Clem. 'We could see steam coming out of his ears.'

'Shut up!' Nick hissed.

'Never seen you so jealous, bro,' Patrick added.

'I have,' John jumped in. 'When I scooped May Grady from under his nose in eighth grade.'

Nick sent his parents a resigned look. 'Seriously, guys, you could've skipped having those three and just had Jess.'

Nick knew that his brothers were trying to lighten the atmosphere and he was grateful. And he had been—was—jealous of Campbell, for the fact that he'd spent the last decade with Clem, that he knew her body intimately, that he'd lived with her and spent all that time with her... He'd only a few weeks and he hardly thought that was fair.

After all, he wasn't a prat.

He'd held his breath while waiting for her to refuse Campbell's stupid proposal—of course he'd known, intellectually, that she'd never say yes—but his heart still jumped around and he could feel hot blood moving through his veins. It was a terrifying revelation to realize how much she meant to him.

He shoved a hand into his hair. 'What now?'

Clem placed two fingers to her temple. 'I need ten minutes with him and then I'm going up to the suite. I've got a pounding headache suddenly.'

'Want me to come with you?' Nick asked, sending Cai, now surrounded by simpering females, another fulminating look. He didn't want her anywhere near him on her own.

Clem shook her head. 'No, I'll be fine. Thanks, though. See you upstairs?'

Nick rubbed his thumb across the back of her hand before

letting her go. It would be so much quicker and cleaner just to wipe the floor with Campbell's face.

And it would make him feel so much better.

Clem leaned her forehead against the door to the suite and took a deep breath. Cai was out of her heart and her mind for ever; she was emotionally free of him and he'd never be more than a memory again. She'd had an explanation of why he was here—he didn't like seeing his woman with another man and he loved her—and why he'd lied to her about the vasectomy—he wanted to tell her but couldn't. His explanations were rubbish and not worth the time thinking about them.

But she had enough dirt on him to gag him; he wouldn't be talking to the press about her again and that was worth putting up with his slimy presence for ten minutes.

Nick was behind this door and he was waiting for her... Was she a fool for wanting this time with him, knowing that they had nowhere to go?

And why did she know, with that fundamental soul-deep feminine wisdom, that being with Nick—sleeping with Nick—would be a turning point in her life, the best and worst thing that could happen to her? It would be wonderful and devastating in equal measure. Wonderful because, well, it was Nick... Devastating because it would be nearly impossible not to fall in love with him if she did.

Could she do this, knowing that she still needed to leave? Shouldn't she just leave things as they were and save herself from the heartbreak of remembering what it was like to be loved by Nick? She knew that Nick wouldn't ask her to stay and realized that if she took this final step leaving him would be torturous.

But didn't she owe herself this space in time, these couple of days of mental and physical pleasure? She'd never known complete and utter abandon in the arms of a man, had never been the complete focus of a man's passion and attention.

She would be with Nick and she deserved that.

Devil and deep blue sea... Either way, she'd walk away feeling as if she'd lost a couple layers of skin.

Clem took a deep breath and opened the door to the suite, which was in total darkness. She slipped off her shoes as she closed the door behind her, groaning when her feet sank into the plush carpet.

'Is it done?'

How was it that she didn't have to explain herself to him? Nick knew that her encounter with Cai had been a watershed moment, that she'd needed to face him and deal with him. 'It's done.'

'Good.'

Nick took two steps before he reached her and then his hands and mouth were everywhere. Clem felt sidewashed by his heat, his power, the sheer passion she could feel radiating off him. As his mouth explored hers, his fingers found the zip of her dress and he pushed the fabric off her shoulders and she stood in front of him, in her high heels and her underwear.

Nick, still dressed, stepped away from her and switched on a side lamp. In the muted light he looked at her; his eyes tracing her face, her body, her legs... His mouth quirked at her sky-high heels and pretty French manicured toes.

'Every man's fantasy,' he murmured, one index finger running across her collarbone. 'So beautiful. Such smooth skin.'

'I need you to...' The words stuck in Clem's throat.

'I will. I'll do it all,' Nick said as he shrugged out of his jacket. He yanked at his collar and pulled his bow tie apart and ripped his shirt open.

Putting his hands on his waist, he sent her a serious look. 'You sure about this?'

Clem shook her head. 'No...yes. I need to be with you.'

She watched his eyes turn to molten silver. 'And I have to have you, Clementine.'

'Then do something, Nick! I'm standing here, practically naked—'

Nick's mouth twitched. 'Not yet.'

Clem gasped while he proceeded to destroy her with a multitude of scintillating somethings.

The next morning Clem rolled over, forced her eyes open and found Nick standing, dressed in jeans and a T-shirt, at the window of the suite. She moved and felt the twinges in her body, a reminder of hours and hours of concentrated attention that Nick had bestowed on her body.

She'd never been so thoroughly loved. No, that was too tame a word...*worshipped* as she had been last night.

'Nick? What are you doing up?' she asked on a huge yawn as she scooted up the bed to lean back against the headboard.

'I've got to get back to Two-B. The rhinos from up north are coming in tomorrow and I have a lot to do.'

'OK. Well, order some coffee and I'll get dressed and then we can go,' Clem said as she slid out of bed. She saw her robe on the foot of the bed and pulled it on.

'Can I watch the rhino relocation?' she asked, walking over to him and putting her hands around his waist. Maybe she could persuade him to come back to bed...

Nick gripped her wrists, pushed her arms to her sides and stepped back. 'Go back to bed, Red.'

Clem heard the hard note in his voice and ignored it. 'Come back to bed with me. Then we can take a shower and then we can get dressed.'

Nick shook his head and swore.

Clem's stomach tightened. 'What's going on, Nick?'

'You're not coming back with me.'

It took Clem a moment before the words registered. 'I beg your pardon?'

She felt the icy fingers of heartbreak and agony tapping their way up her spine.

'I think you should just go back to London or New York...
there's no point in you coming back to Two-B.'

No point? She looked at the bed they'd just shared, the pillows on the floor, the half ripped away sheet.

'I'm sorry, I thought the deal was that I'd come back to
Two-B with you for a couple of days before I returned home.'
She kept her voice very controlled, very calm.

'That deal is off.'

Clem lifted her eyebrows, aware that her heart had reached
her toes. 'Why?'

'Last night was a mistake,' Nick said, leaning his shoulder
into the wall, his eyes shuttered. 'As we knew it would be.'

Clem tucked her hands beneath her arms so that he
wouldn't see them shaking. She made herself ask the question, just to make sure. 'Is this about Cai? About what happened last night?'

Nick shook his head. 'It's never been about him. From the
first moment you stepped off that plane and looked at me, it's
only ever been about us.'

Clem felt as if she were in a flimsy life raft in the middle
of twenty-foot seas. She had no idea what to do but she knew
with certainty that she was about to drown. 'So, what's the
problem?'

Nick jammed his hands into his pockets. 'Clem, last night
we scratched an itch, can we not just leave it at that?'

Clem's eyes flashed and her voice wavered. 'Don't you
dare! That's not fair, Nick. The least you can be right now is
honest with me.'

Nick banged his hand down on the table next to him. He
scrubbed his face with his hand. This was why he avoided
relationships; he felt as if he'd been tossed back five years,
arguing with Terra again. Or trying to sort out his siblings'
hysterics. Or his dad's temper, his mom's tears...

He could see that she was utterly at sea. He didn't blame
her—he was acting like a jerk but he didn't seem to be able

to help it. Admittedly, he was exhausted, having spent most of the night loving Clem and the rest of the time watching her sleep. But it wasn't tiredness that had his heart clenching. No, he could lay the blame for that firmly at the feet of his feelings for this complicated woman.

They were too deep, too intense already. He couldn't afford to let her stay another day because in one night she'd stolen his body, his heart was in her hands and his soul was about to surrender to her too.

He was too close to love and its sidekicks, fear and pain. Loving would be a series of monumental risks, none of which he was prepared to take.

If she stayed one day, one hour longer he'd be lost...

'Nick—'

When she looked at him like that, he just wanted to take her in his arms and say, *To hell with it all.* Annoyed that she had so much power over him, he felt his temper heat. It had been simmering since last night, sparked by the jealousy he felt when Campbell had arrived.

It was ridiculous... He'd known her for four weeks! Four weeks was nothing...

'We can work this out,' Clem said.

'There is nothing to work out, Red. We slept together. It's done. Let's move on.'

'Move on how?'

'Back to our lives. Go and be whatever you are and I'll do the same.'

Clem looked at her clenched hands. 'What am I, Nick?'

The words, propelled by fear and pure jerk-ness, rocketed out of his mouth. 'You're a flighty, irresponsible socialite who has the means and opportunity to flit around the world like a pretty butterfly. You don't know anything about the bush—'

'I've been learning—' Clem protested, his words striking her like bullets.

'You've got the attention span of a gnat!'

'That's not fair,' Clem whispered, wrapping her arms around her middle. 'That's so not fair.'

It wasn't, he knew it wasn't, but what could he tell her? Stay with me, be with me, knowing that in a couple of months, a couple of years, she'd leave and he'd be left at Two-B with only his ripped apart heart for company?

'Are you telling me that you want to stay at Two-B with me?' he scoffed.

Clem shrugged. 'I want the choice! I want you to talk to me, I don't want to be dismissed as if I'm a stupid, useless ditz who you're suddenly tired of.'

That was fair comment but he couldn't afford to play fair. He forced himself to continue, feeling more like a worm with every word. 'Where did you think we were going? Did you honestly think that we had a future? You'd last three months at Two-B before you'd bail, whining about the fact that you couldn't get a manicure or go and see a movie.'

'I haven't asked you for anything other than a couple of days!' Clem protested. 'And you're being spectacularly unfair and unreasonable! Apart from those first couple of days at Two-B, and the other day, I've never once nagged or whined or complained. I did everything you asked me to! It's not my fault that I grew up in a world so different from yours but you can't say I didn't try!'

'Terra grew up in my world and she left,' Nick said in a monotonous voice. Why couldn't she understand that he couldn't live through that again?

'I am not Terra!' Clem shouted back, tears streaming down her face. 'For goodness' sake, Nick, I stayed in a useless relationship for ten years because I was too stubborn to give in or give up! Why can't you see that? When I decide I want something, I don't give up and I don't walk out.'

'Yeah, but there are some subtle differences here, Princess. He was a rock star and you have houses in New York, LA and London. When you're bored with one, you could jump on your private jet and find some entertainment at the other. At Two-B, there's nowhere to run when you get bored and I'm sure as hell not going to be your punchbag. I don't want to feel this way, Clem, not for you and not for anyone. Because I don't trust easy and I don't trust quick.'

His unspoken *and I don't trust you* hovered between them, silent but as tangible as her tears.

I don't trust you not to leave and I don't trust myself not to make you the centre, the axis of my world, Nick silently admitted. *My everything.*

Clem sank down onto the couch and dropped her head. She couldn't, wouldn't win this argument. Nick had decided that she wasn't suited to his life and, despite doing everything she possibly could to show him that she wasn't a flighty girl any more, he still, fundamentally, saw her as one.

This man, the one she thought knew her best, didn't seem to know her at all. She knew that he couldn't—wouldn't—love her but she, at least, had thought that he understood her. 'I really thought you were the one person who saw me for the person I am. I cannot believe how wrong I was about you.'

How very, very wrong. Devastated. Annihilated. Flattened. Clem couldn't think which word suited her best. It was a bigger betrayal than she had imagined.

Clem swallowed and thought that, before she walked out of his life for ever, that she should make sure that she was crystal clear on what was happening.

'You're calling it...whatever the hell "it" is...over, aren't you?'

'I think it's the most sensible thing to do,' Nick replied. 'Call it quits before either of us falls too deep and gets hurt.'

Bit late for that, Clem thought.

'Besides, I'm nothing more than your rebound fling, your stepping stone to someone bigger and brighter. Just next time, choose a guy who can sing and play music, OK?'

Clem wiped her hands over her tear-stained face.

'It's been an…education but it's time for all our lives to go back to normal.' Nick's bored tone sliced hard and deep.

OK, he'd said more than enough and far more than she needed to take. It was time she stood up for herself and what she wanted.

Clem stood up and looked him in the eye. 'I think you've been cruel and nasty. I bought my ticket, Nick. I always knew that I had to go. We could've had a fun week and you could've put me on a plane and wished me well. Instead, you've sliced me and diced me.'

Nick started to speak but Clem silenced him with a hard look. 'No, it's my turn to speak. I can deal with you not loving me. I can't make you feel something for me that isn't there. But I can't forgive you for still seeing me as a pathetic, stupid princess without a brain between her ears and a heart that can't be hurt. Yes, I was spoilt—probably still am in some ways—and I made some stupid choices. But I'm not Terra, I'm not a vapid society girl. I am Clem and I deserved to be loved because I'm a damn good bet. But if you can't see any of that then we don't have anything more to say to each other.'

Clem jumped up and stalked over to the telephone. When the concierge answered, she spoke in her coolest, coldest society voice.

'This is Clem Copeland. Is Cai Campbell staying in this hotel? Connect me, please.'

The muscle in Nick's jaw jumped. 'Are you going back to him?'

'You are an idiot for even thinking that,' Clem told him. 'Cai? Wake up! Where is your jet? Call the pilot and tell him I'm on my way…he's taking me to London. No? Do I need to tell the press about the plastic surgery you had on your…? I didn't think so. No, you cannot come with me. I've had enough of men to last me a lifetime. Find your own way home.'

Clem banged down the telephone and sent Nick a long, lost look. 'Goodbye, Nick.'

Using the last vestiges of willpower and emotional strength she could find, she walked to the bathroom and locked the door behind her. She thought she knew what a broken heart felt like, she thought as she sank to the floor and curled up in a ball, but she hadn't a clue until now.

In Soho, Clem climbed out of a taxi and, because she was a little early for her lunch date, decided to walk the last block to the restaurant where she was meeting Jason.

She wrapped her scarf around her neck and shivered. She'd never been so cold, inside and out. The temperature at Two-B would be scorching today; she knew because she was a hopeless, love-struck twit who'd checked.

And, despite her resolve not to think about him, she was off and running. Nick would probably be in his office right now... Her heart moaned and she fought the urge to double over in pain. This would never happen again, she promised herself. Never. Ever. Again. The pain was indescribable, the constant gnawing of wolves eating her innards.

A month...she'd known Nick a scant four weeks and yet he'd managed to rip her heart right out of her chest. She had all the symptoms—the waves of pain that constantly dunked her, the terrible ache in her stomach, the relentless insomnia. She couldn't eat, she couldn't sleep and she wandered around London like a ghost.

It wasn't the first time she was venturing out of her flat—she'd taken to aimlessly walking—but she still felt a little shocked and overwhelmed by the noise, the people and the traffic. It was a normal grey, dismal day in London and she wanted the sun, the cry of the fish eagle, the laugh of a hyena.

Nicks arms, Nick's smile, Nick's everything. She wanted to go home.

Jason stood up as she approached and kissed her on the

cheek. Unwinding her scarf, she sat down and shrugged off her coat.

He shook his head at her red-rimmed eyes, her sunken cheeks. 'You've dropped the weight you picked up, and more. Are you eating?'

'Yes.'

'Liar.' Jason shook his head again and, without consulting Clem, ordered the soup special for both of them. 'Clem, I left you in Africa with a bruised heart. I didn't expect you to come home with a broken one.'

'Tell me about it.'

'What happened?'

Clem lifted her shoulders in a sad shrug. 'Does it matter? It's over, whatever it was.'

'Did you sleep together?' Jason asked.

Clem propped her chin into the palm of her hand. 'Yes.'

Jason winced. 'Now I understand why you're walking around looking like Morticia Addams. You love him; you wouldn't have slept with him otherwise.'

The knife that resided under her ribcage jabbed her. 'Yes, I fell in love. Totally, fundamentally, soul-suckingly in love.'

Jason cursed and leaned forward. 'Seriously?'

'As a heart attack.'

'And him?'

'He thinks we're too different, that I could never last on Two-B. He decided to call it quits before it went too deep.'

'Except that you had already fallen.'

'Yeah.' Clem took her serviette and pulled it through her fingers. 'The vultures were back outside my door today.'

Jason nodded. 'Your ending with Nick was too abrupt and they know there is more to it...and they'll keep hounding you until you close that door. Do an interview, answer some questions and the interest will die off.'

Clem wrinkled her nose. 'I'll think about it.'

Jason leaned back in his chair. 'So, what's the next step? With you? What are you going to do?'

'Apart from dying of a broken heart?' Clem asked, her chin in her hand. 'I don't know. I'm going mad, so I need to keep busy.'

Jason leaned back as the waiter placed the soup bowls in front of them. 'If I had to ask you what would you like to do the most, can you answer me?'

Clem nodded slowly. 'Maybe. I have this idea that won't go away...'

'Well, tell me about it while you eat something.' He pointed his spoon at Clem and narrowed his eyes when she hesitated. 'Do not even think about arguing with me!'

Clem ate. And told him what she thought she might like to do with the rest of her Nick-empty life.

A month after Clem left, Nick walked into a restaurant in Melville, Johannesburg and saw Jessica's wave. He smiled when he saw that all three of his brothers were seated at the table with her and wondered when last they'd all had lunch together...it certainly hadn't been for many, many years. His fault entirely...as so much was.

Another pity party, Sherwood?

Nick walked up to the table, dropped a kiss on Jess's cheek and greeted his brothers. He took the seat with his back to the door and opened the menu Chris handed him and stared at the offerings. Food, like much else, held little appeal for him since Clem had left but he knew he needed it to function so he ordered a simple BLT and tried to work up the enthusiasm needed to choke it down.

He tried to listen to Chris and John's discussion about something political and, not caring, switched to tune into Jess and Patrick's conversation and couldn't make head or tail of that either.

He wanted to go back to Two-B. He'd been in the city for six hours and he was already feeling claustrophobic.

Nick heard a shriek of female laughter and his head whipped around. Three stylish women sat in the corner, two tables down, and when the blonde caught his eye she gave him a slow, sexy, deliberate wink.

Yeah, thanks but no. Bottom line, you're not Clem…

Nick excused himself from the table and walked to the men's room, which was thankfully empty. He gripped the edge of a basin with both hands and stared down at the rusty ring around the plughole. He had to get over her. Get past this full-blown mind-body-heart attack, the constant knot in his stomach, the black hole in his heart. He had to start eating properly, he needed more than intermittent sleep and he needed sex. The blonde in the corner…

Nick's stomach lurched and he stared at his wild, tired eyes in the mirror. OK, he'd start with eating and sleeping and when he got that right, he'd move on up to sex…in about ten years or so.

When Nick made it back to the table, he saw that Jabu was sitting next to Jess, his arm around her shoulders. 'What are you doing here?' Nick asked. 'I thought you had a dentist appointment.'

'Sorted,' Jabu replied.

'And Jabs is family; he's never needed an invitation to join us!' Jess snapped.

'I know that. He's my brother as much as you guys are. I just asked why he was here,' Nick grumbled. He pointed a finger at Jabu. 'You can fly home; I'm going to have a beer.'

Nick ordered his beer and, turning back to the table, saw five faces looking at him. He rolled his eyes and caught a clue. 'So, what is this? An intervention?' he barked.

Jess, still the gutsiest of his siblings, took a breath and spoke first. 'This is us, telling you that we are worried about you. And we don't care if you tell us to mind our own business; we're your family and we love you, so deal with it. And we won't let you go back into hiding so don't even think about threatening us with that!'

Nick held up his fingers and made a cross. 'Calm down. I'm not going anywhere and I'm not going to go back into hiding. I'm fine, OK? Seriously.'

'You are not fine,' Jabu snapped. 'You are miserable and short and scratchy and a pain. Will you just call the woman already and get her back here?'

Nick's laugh was hollow. 'Yeah...no. Why should I?'

'Because she made you happy.' Patrick used his psychiatrist's voice and Nick wanted to punch him. 'She's a nice person, Nicholas, and good for you.'

'You met her once. How the hell would you know?' Nick snapped.

Jess reached into her bag and passed Nick a note. He looked down at Clem's writing and his hand started to shake.

Hey Jess,
I was clearing out my stuff from the LA house and I found these boxes of shoes...some are brand new. I thought you might like them...we're the same size, aren't we?
   Enjoy them! Sorry I had to leave before we could become better friends.
Take care
Clem xxx
PS Have had quite a bit of time on my hands so I did some shopping. Just some small gifts for your parents to say thank you for a wonderful evening. Please deliver them for me.

Nick handed the note back to Jess and took a sip of his beer, not realizing that a muscle in his cheek was jumping. 'Nice of her.'

'A leather-bound copy of Dickens's *Christmas Carol* for Mom, an artist's beret from a vintage clothes shop for Dad as a joke. Thoughtful, kind presents,' Jess said.

Nick's hand shook as he lifted his beer. 'As I said, nice of her. I never said she couldn't be nice.'

'Yeah,' Jabu commented. 'Like it was nice of her to donate her entire pay cheque from that crazy reality show to the foundation. Seven hundred and fifty thousand?'

Hell, in the scheme of things he'd forgotten about the original deal they'd struck. The foundation had three-quarters of a million in their coffers…in dollars. They could do some excellent work with that type of money.

Nice but…Nick let out a breath. It didn't make a damn bit of difference; she was still thousands of miles away because he had told her to go. And because he hadn't done a thing to bring her back.

'Look, Clem wasn't cut out for living at Two-B. She was useless!' Nick ground out, using the only excuse he could to convince them he'd been right to let her go. It wasn't as if he could say, *I sent her away because I'm terrified of what I was feeling for her.*

'She wasn't that helpful, she doesn't understand what it takes to run a reserve, she couldn't tell the difference between a water buck and a kudu!' Nick dug his hole deeper and he saw the scepticism on their faces. He sighed, he knew it sounded lame. He sounded stupid…he hated sounding stupid. But stupid, he was coming to accept, he definitely was.

Chris leaned back in his seat and looked at Jabu and his siblings. 'Well, doesn't that just make sense? We get it now. How could you possibly love a woman who can't tell the difference, after being there for just a month, between two antelope species?'

Nick glared at him. 'You don't understand!'

'Too right I don't! So what—did you draw up a list of criteria for the woman you fall in love with? Has to have a degree in wildlife management...'

'Minor in Ornithology...' John added.

'A degree in animal medicine would be nice...' Patrick added his two cents' worth.

Nick scowled at Jabu. 'You have anything pertinent to add?'

'Their points are valid; what are you looking for in a partner? A worker for Two-B or someone who makes you happy?' Jabu shrugged. 'And may I point out the obvious?'

'No, you may not,' Nick muttered.

'You had all that in Terra and you were never as happy with her as you are with Clem.' Jabu sent him a sympathetic smile. 'Nick, pull yourself together and do something about her, for all of our sakes! Please?'

Nick opened his mouth to argue...and snapped it shut again. He shook his head and pushed his chair back from the table. Draining his beer as he stood, he placed it on the table, turned on his heel and walked out of the restaurant.

In his car, he rested his forehead against the steering wheel and cursed. His family was right, damn it. Letting her leave, pushing her away was, to date, the stupidest, most asinine, chronically pathetic decision of his life. He loved her, he missed her and he'd sent her away because he had the courage of a fainting goat. He'd been scared of her leaving, frightened that he couldn't live without her and guess what? She had left and he couldn't live without her.

So what the hell was he supposed to do now?

His mobile chirped and he picked it up from the passenger seat and frowned at the BBM from Jess.

So, does your storming out of the restaurant mean that you're going to bring her home? BTW, it's only a couple of months until Christmas, we'd like her as a sister-in-law. An early Christmas present.

Jess...Nick had to grin at her message. Subtle as a buffalo.

CHAPTER TWELVE

Luella Dawson's blog:

OK, people, it's been a while since I posted about the The Crazy Cs and I have news! Let's do a quick recap. We last saw Nick and Clem at the ball, where they were smoking up the dance floor. I, for one, was waiting for them to spontaneously combust from the heat they generated...then Cai made a spectacular entrance and proposed.

Nick disappeared first, then Cai, then Clem. Since then, nearly four weeks later, and despite the media frenzy, we've heard nothing.

None of them are available for comment—not even Cai, who'd be interviewed by a warthog if it got him some publicity. Clem left Two-B and Nick threatened to shoot the next journalist who called, e-mailed or texted him. They left us hanging, people!

But I have a present for the boys and girls...

My people called Clem's people, as we do (with little expectation) looking for an interview and Clem agreed to appear on my show. This will be the first interview with any journalist since the drama and, if I understand her correctly, the only interview she will be giving in the foreseeable future.

*Of course I said no...kidding! Clem will be on my
show on October 5th. Tune in then!*

C‍LEM sat in the green room and thought that her heart was
going to bang out of her chest. She reached for Jason's hand
and gripped his fingers.

'Am I doing the right thing?' she demanded, her smoky
eyes frantic.

'We discussed this Clem, this is your way of closing this
door...'

Clem shook her head. 'I think it's a mistake!'

Jason nodded to a staffer who appeared in the door. 'Too
late now, it's time.'

Clem bit her lip and clung to Jason before walking off with
the staffer. Anyone, Jason thought with a wry smile, would
think she was going off to the executioner.

He whipped his mobile out of his pocket and opened up
his contacts. He jumped when Clem poked her head back
around the door. 'You didn't call him and tell him about this,
did you?'

'Who?' he asked, holding the mobile against his leg.

'Nick. You said you wouldn't.'

'I haven't called him, Clem,' Jason replied.

'Because if he wanted me then he would've called me by
now,' Clem said, her voice edged with despair.

'Miss Copeland, we're going to be late.'

'I haven't called him, Clem,' Jason shouted after her. Well,
he hadn't... He slammed his mobile closed and tossed it onto
the coffee table.

Damn it, he'd been so close.

Nick rubbed a towel over his wet head and considered his op-
tions on how to approach Clem. He was planning to call her
father today to find out where she was and then he'd book the

first flight out; he couldn't say what he needed to say on the phone or by e-mail… No, he needed to do this face to face.

He owed her that much. Besides, she could disconnect a call or not reply to an e-mail.

He pulled on a pair of shorts as his BlackBerry buzzed, alerting him to a new e-mail message. His heart leapt at the subject line and considered himself an absolute anorak for plugging Clem into Google alerts after he'd left the restaurant in Jo'burg yesterday. This was the first new alert he'd had and he opened the link.

Don't forget my interview with Clem Copeland in my New York studio. Luella Dawson blog.

Luella Dawson—wasn't she the same person who'd interviewed Cai and Clem? Nick glanced at his watch, calculated the time difference and yelped… It was due to start! He hopped over the couch to grab the remote off the coffee table and hit the buttons and there she was, dressed in solid black. A polo neck under a tunic over tights and knee-high boots. Her locket glinted under the studio lights and Nick leaned forward to get closer to her.

Her hair was longer and clipped back from her face and she was still too skinny… Had she been eating at all since she'd left?'

Luella and Clem took their seats and Nick held his fist to his mouth, hardly listening as they complimented each other on their outfits and hair.

'So, Clem, the last time you were here you vomited into a rather nice bag.'

Clem smiled and Nick's stomach turned over. 'I did.'

'But, let's start our chat off with what everyone wants to know. What's the status of The Crazy Cs?'

'Cai and I are over.'

'We all know that there are degrees of over, especially in Hollywood.'

'There will never be any chance of reconciliation between us,' Clem answered in a firm voice.

Good to know, Nick thought.

Luella glanced down at her notes. 'Are you prepared to give us details of whether there was a financial settlement between you?'

'Come on, Luella,' Clem chided.

'The public is interested.' Luella wasn't chastised at all.

Clem shrugged. 'I took my clothes, my mother's furniture and art, and I kept my flat in London. That's it.'

Luella looked gob-smacked. 'No cash settlement? You were with him for a decade!'

Clem crossed her legs. 'I don't need his money, Luella.'

'I know that you have an income from a trust your mother set up for you but would you consider a job?'

'Why not? Hard work doesn't scare me.'

Luella raised her ruthlessly plucked eyebrows. 'It doesn't?'

No, it didn't, Nick realized. She'd never been afraid to get her hands dirty, to put in the hours.

'So, are you on good terms with Cai?' Luella probed.

He felt, rather than saw, Clem's internal eye roll. 'I wish him nothing but happiness, but he is a part of my past and I've moved on.'

Luella tipped her head. 'So, what have you been up to since you left The Baobab and Buffalo Lodge?'

Clem smiled. 'This and that.'

'Your PA sent us an update. Apparently you're studying?'

Clem crossed her legs again. 'I have registered for a couple of correspondence courses and intend to get my degree in business management.'

'Are you joining your father's company?'

'No. I'm thinking about setting up a foundation, in my mum's name, to establish a rhino sanctuary in both Africa and on the sub-Indian continent, looking at caring for and raising baby rhinos whose mothers have been poached in the wild.'

Luella looked astounded. 'Why on earth do you want to do that?'

'Rescuing that baby rhino at Two-B had a big impact on me.'

The Princess was gone, Nick thought. This confident woman on the screen was taking responsibility for her life, trying to make a difference, to throw her energy into something she believed in. Maybe he'd sparked her interest in the cause but he could hear the passion in her voice... She was just perfect.

'So, we'll come back to your future plans in a moment,' Luella said. 'Is London home now?'

The camera zoomed in on Clem's face and Nick saw the flash of pain in her eyes and he sucked in his breath. 'Yes...'

Luella, good interviewer that she was, picked up the hesitation he heard in Clem's voice. She leaned forward and looked intently at Clem. 'From the footage of your time in Africa, we all thought that you'd found the place you loved best. And it wasn't London.'

Clem's eyes deepened and she licked her bottom lip and Nick—and probably everybody else in the world watching—knew that Luella had pierced through her reserve to the vulnerability beneath.

'Maybe.'

Images of Clem and him—courtesy of the reality show—slid onto the wide screens behind their heads and Nick felt his eyes sting. Clem, her head resting on the back of the lounger, bare feet up on the railing of the deck, laughing up at him, her face open and happy. Both of them grinning like crazy at each other after they'd rescued the baby rhino, Clem with bed head in the morning, looking at him over her coffee cup. A magnificent photograph of Clem's wide smile as she stood on the red carpet just after he'd told her that he preferred her muddy and dirty.

She looked as if she belonged here in his house, with him.

Hell, she did and it was time he did something about it. Nick grabbed his mobile and dialled.

'Hoped I'd be hearing from you,' Jason said, his voice smug.

'Tell them to Skype me in to the show. Do you think they'd do that?'

'Do lions roar? Grab your computer, then don't move,' Jason said, thoroughly overexcited.

'It's right here, next to me.' Nick flipped the lid, powered it up and glanced at the TV screen again. He tossed his mobile on the table and took a seat on the couch, the computer on the coffee table in front of him and his eyes on the TV screen.

Well, it was time that he showed her, and himself, that he did have a little more courage than a fainting goat.

Not much, but some.

Clem wished she could glance at her watch to see how much time she had left on this torture session. It was worse than sorting the waste for recycling at Two-B. They'd just come back from the advertisement break and she wondered what had caused the buzz of excitement amongst the crew and why Luella had gone into a private huddle with a producer.

Another celebrity scandal, she presumed. It didn't matter. After this she was done with being a celebrity or anything close to one. She'd just be Clem Copeland again and she couldn't wait. Nothing would make her happier... Oh, liar, she could cope with being back at Two-B but that wasn't going to happen.

It had been four weeks of complete and utter silence. He hadn't changed his mind and she had no expectation of him doing so.

Luella put her hand on Clem's knee and she jumped. 'Sorry, miles away.'

'And we're back in three, two, one...'

Luella smiled at the camera and turned back to Clem. 'So, Clem, we've had quite a few texts and e-mails from our viewers asking questions and we're getting quite a few Skype calls. Would you mind answering some questions from our viewers?'

Clem lifted her hands. Anything to get this done. 'Sure.'

Luella turned to a screen to her left where a text message appeared. 'You and Nick seemed to have a real connection. Do you talk?'

Clem swallowed. Of course they were going to ask about Nick, it was to be expected. But what could she say? *I'm madly in love with the man but he doesn't want me?*

'Nick is a very busy man and this is a crazy time for him. We don't talk that often.'

Like never.

'Pity,' Luella murmured. 'We have a Skype call from Jade in California.'

'Hi, Clem.' A perky, busty blonde waved at her from the screen. 'I love your fashion style. Who are your favourite designers?'

Clem sighed her relief. Easy one. 'I don't have any favourite designers...I love them all, as my closet will happily tell you. I have outfits from everybody, including second-hand shops. I love vintage dresses and hats.'

'Thank you, Jade. Another Skype call. Hannah in...Hong Kong?'

Hannah in Hong Kong was tiny and gorgeous with jet-black hair and a bright red mouth. 'Are you in love with Nick?'

Oooh, solid blow. Clem gripped her locket and tried to smile. 'I think that's too personal a question.'

Luella's eyes flashed with excitement. 'The calls and texts and e-mails are flooding in. Another Skype call, Clem.'

'I'm quite interested in getting a definitive answer to the last question,' a deep and disturbingly familiar voice said and Clem's head shot up to see Nick on the big screen behind Luella.

'Hey, Red.'

Clem leaned forward and put her fingers to her mouth. 'Nick...what?'

'Well?'

Clem shook her head, confused. 'I'm sorry...what are you doing?'

'Trying to find out whether you love me or not.' Nick lifted his coffee cup to his lips as he waited for her answer and Clem saw that his fingers were shaking. Seeing that he was nervous—her strong, steady, confident man—had her eyebrows lifting. Her heart felt as if it were about to free fall out of her chest.

'Is my answer that important to you?' Clem managed to get the words out, and in the right order.

'Well, I wouldn't be asking it on a TV show if I didn't think it was.'

Then Clem remembered their last conversation and her eyes, and voice, cooled. 'Why are you doing this, Nick? Haven't you done enough?'

Nick blew out his cheeks and nodded. 'Look, I don't blame you for being angry but can I at least explain?'

Clem leaned back, crossed her arms and tipped her head. 'Go on then.'

'Now?'

'I'm listening.'

'So am I,' Luella interjected.

'And the rest of the world,' Nick complained. 'Look, Red, I'll catch a plane, we'll sit down and thrash this out.'

Clem shook her head. 'No time like the present.'

Nick narrowed his grey shadowed eyes at her. 'You're doing this to punish me, aren't you?'

'You're the one that called in to the show,' Clem pointed out. 'If you don't have anything pertinent to say then I'm sure that there are other callers.' She cocked her head. 'So, do you want to tell me why it is important for you to know whether I love you or not?'

Nick shoved his hand into his hair. 'Because I think it's all that would fill up the hole I have in my life, my heart, my home.'

'If that's true, then why did you boot me out of your life like I was nothing?'

'Because you were everything.'

Clem swallowed. 'I don't understand. You said we didn't have a future, that I wasn't suited to your life, that I couldn't stick it out. That I was a stupid society girl who should go back to her parties and pleasure.'

'I know what I said, Clem, and I'm sorry for it. All of it.' Nick rubbed his forehead. When he spoke again his voice was terse with frustration and worry. 'What do you want me to say? Do you want me to say that I was bone-deep scared of what I was feeling—do feel—for you?'

'And are you? Scared?'

'Yes! You turned my life on its head and I thought that if I sent you away then I could go back to normality. But I found out that normality sucks. And yes, what I feel for you scares the hell out of me!'

'Then why are you here, talking to me?'

'I thought I could live without you, but I can't. I thought that I could stop these crazy feelings for you, but I can't.' Nick placed his forearms on his thighs and leaned forward. His eyes were steel-grey with emotion and the saliva in Clem's mouth disappeared. 'I can't, Red. Anything. Everything. Not without you.'

Clem's mouth twitched as she tried to hide her enormous smile. 'So, ask me again.'

Nick looked perplexed. 'Ask you what?'

'Ask her whether she loves you or not,' Luella told Nick.

The puzzlement on Nick's face cleared. 'Oh, OK. So, Red. Are you in love with me?'

'Of course I am. I would've told you at the time but you sent me away without allowing me to explain that I needed to go but I would come back, if that's what you wanted.'

Joy diffused over Nick's features and the cameras, Luella and the world disappeared. 'Well, I can be extraordinarily stupid on occasion.'

Clem smiled. 'You can.'

She lifted up her hand as if to touch him and noticed that Nick caught the movement. Nick's eyes glinted with passion. 'And, knowing that, I'm anxious to know when you are going to get your skinny butt on a plane and come home?'

'I'm not.' Clem lifted up a hand at his protest. 'You still haven't given me any reason to.'

'I've just poured out my heart to you!' Nick protested.

'You've told me that you have crazy feelings for me. That could mean anything from indigestion to frustration,' Clem said.

Luella rolled her eyes. 'Nicholas! Stop being thick and tell her that you love her!'

Nick raked a hand through his hair. 'Jeez, Red, you're going to make me say it...on national—international—TV?'

Clem grinned. 'Well, I did.'

'But you're a girl!'

Clem's mouth dropped open and she shook her head at Luella, who leaned forward, tears glistening in her eyes.

'We won't listen, Nick, I promise,' Luella assured him.

'Yeah, right. Clementine...'

'Yes?'

Nick dropped his head and looked down at his hands. Clem

held her breath and waited until he lifted his head again and gasped at the emotion churning in those amazing eyes. Love, hope…lust, but mostly love. For her.

'I don't know how to tell you how much I love you, how much I've missed you. Four weeks and you turned my life upside down, but I want you to keep doing that for…I don't know, the next sixty, seventy years? That enough of a commitment for you?'

Clem felt, and ignored, the tears on her cheeks. 'That works for me. I'm catching the first plane I can.'

'I can come to you,' Nick offered.

Clem shook her head. 'I need to come home, Nick.'

'Then come, sweetheart. Just get here as quick as you can,' Nick said, his voice low.

This wasn't a time for tears, Clem told herself. She was loved and in love. And she was on TV.

Tossing her head, she blinked, sent Nick her naughtiest smile and his eyes crinkled.

'I know that look, that smile. What do you want, Red?'

'Do you know that it's my birthday next week?'

Nick leaned back and placed his arm along the back of the couch. He looked relaxed and happy. So happy. 'I'd heard a rumour.'

Clem's eyes sparkled as she drank him in. 'You know what I'd like for a present?'

'A diamond engagement ring? A baby? Shares in Two-B?' Nick's voice sounded flippant but, in his eyes, she could see that he was offering any and all. When Nick committed, he did it with everything he had.

Clem placed her hand on her heart. 'I'd prefer an emerald, I don't need the shares and I'd love a baby at some point. But my request is a lot simpler.'

'OK…'

'Since I intend spending an inordinate amount of time

with you in the immediate future, can you please fix the spring in Landy?'

Nick's wicked grin flashed. 'I said I love you, not that you weren't a pain in my butt...'

Clem laughed and threw one of Luella's very expensive cushions at the screen.

Nick paced the small area in front of the International Arrivals and frowned at the electronic board above his head. He knew that Clem's flight had landed—it said so—but what the sodding hell was taking so long? Where was she? It had been thirty-six hours since the TV show, fourteen when he'd last spoken to her... He grabbed his mobile and dialled her number again.

'Where are you?' he muttered after she yelped her hello.

'Trying to find my luggage.'

'Forget your luggage, you don't need clothes,' Nick growled. 'Just get out here.'

He heard Clem huff, heard the clunk of a suitcase. 'Got it. Where are you?'

'Where I've been for the *past six hours*, right by Arrivals. Hurry up!'

'Don't stop talking to me. Don't go away,' Clem said, her voice vibrating with emotion. He could hear the tears in her voice, knew that he was close to the edge himself.

'Last chance, Red,' he told her, his voice hoarse. 'You walk through those doors and I'm never letting you go. Do you understand that?'

'Walk through those doors? I'm flying!' Clem said and she was. Nick looked up as she belted through the door in tight blue jeans and running on ridiculously high boots, dragging a small suitcase behind her. Nick pushed past a suit and stepped into her path, swinging her up as she fell into his arms.

Then her legs were around his waist, his face was in her hair and Clem was sobbing against his neck.

'Shh, sweetheart. I've got you.' Nick held her with one arm and rubbed his other hand up and down her back. 'I'm here, you're here, it's all good. Shh.'

Clem's arms tightened around his neck and he could feel her tears sliding down the collar of his shirt. 'I've missed you so much.'

'I missed you too,' Nick said as she lifted her head. He let her drop down his body and held her as she found her feet. Digging his hands into her hair, he tipped her face up to look at him. 'I'm so sorry for what I said...I know you. I do know you.'

Clem bit her bottom lip. 'Are you sure? I need you to see me clearly...not as I was but who I am, now.'

'You're Clem and perfect as you are. Funny, big-hearted, loyal, passionate, stubborn. I see you, sweetheart, I do. I love who you are today and I'll love who you are always.'

Clem blinked and tears ran. 'Why didn't you call—I kept hoping you would—'

Nick thumbed the moisture off her cheek. 'I thought I'd get over you...gave myself a week, then another. Then I thought I needed more time but, instead of missing you less, I just ended up missing you more. I swear I was coming for you. I was trying to work out how but I was coming for you.'

Clem reached into her bag for a tissue and hiccupped a sob when Nick took the tissue from her hand and gently wiped her tears away. She kept her eyes locked on his and saw the truth within them. He did see her, know her, for exactly who and what she was. Relieved, she reached up and kissed his mouth, before giving him a wobbly but wide smile. 'OK, then. So, I'm here. What now?'

Nick grinned at her. 'Well, I think we should pick up where we left off, before I acted like an ass.'

Clem laughed as he grabbed her suitcase with one hand and her hand with the other.

'Oh? So that's why I travelled all this way? For sex?' she teased as they walked towards the exit.

Nick stopped and looked at her. 'Absolutely. But also because I intend making sure that you are insanely happy for the rest of your life. That OK with you?'

Clem nodded, tears welling again. 'So OK.'

'Now, can we please find a bed so that I can *show* you how much I love you?'

It was dawn and Clem woke up to the raucous morning chorus of the birds, Nick's arm banded around her waist. It was two days before her birthday and she was in Nick's room—her room—at Two-B. She had a million things to do, she realized, lifting Nick's hand and slipping out of bed. She smiled down at him as he shifted, looking for her, and slid back into sleep. He should be tired, Clem thought, since he'd devoted the last week to showing her—in the most delightful ways possible—how much he loved and adored her.

She pulled on a short robe and walked to the kitchen and made herself a cup of coffee. Nick's entire family, and her father, was flying in today to spend her birthday weekend with them at Two-B. Miraculously, the private villa was unoccupied for three days and the Sherwood family would stay there while her father would move into their spare room.

Taking her coffee onto the deck, she wondered how she felt about sleeping with Nick with her father in the room next door. They'd probably have to stop making love in the shower for a while...

Clem grinned and leaned on the railing, looking over the waterhole. Her grin turned into a wide smile when she felt Nick's hand on her back and she handed him her cup of coffee to share.

'Why are you up so early and why are you grinning like that?' Nick asked, standing in his boxers, looking fit and rumpled and so sexy he took her breath away.

'I was thinking that we might have to stop doing it in the shower when my father arrives.'

Nick nuzzled her neck. 'Uh, no. We'll just have to be quiet.'

'Eland at the waterhole,' Clem told him as he wound his arms around her waist.

Clem felt him shaking his head. 'Nyala.'

'Damn it! I thought I had that one,' she muttered.

'Lucky I want a wife, not a game ranger,' Nick said, his voice full of laughter.

Clem dropped her head sideways and looked up at him. 'Is that a proposal?'

'It's a suggestion. The proposal would be dependent on whether you're open to the idea or not.'

Clem cocked her head as he stepped away from her. 'You still have doubts that I love you and that I'd say yes?'

Nick shoved his hand into his hair. 'Not that you love me but whether this is enough for you. I live in the middle of nowhere, Clem, seeing the same people day in and day out.'

'Well, I'm going to be pretty busy studying and getting the baby rhino orphanage up and running and when I'm not doing that, I'm sure that you'll have stuff for me to do so I'm not going to be bored.'

'I know, but…'

'Nick, stop worrying. If I get cabin fever I promise I'll talk to you about it. I'm a talker, so you will always know where I stand. I've found new friends in Hannah and Megan on the reserve and if I need a city fix, I'll go to Jo'burg and hang out with your mother and sister. We can take the occasional holiday. I love the reserve and I love you. Trust me, I'll be fine and we'll be fine.'

'I meant what I said; I'm never letting you go. I'd give up everything else before I let you go.'

Clem bit her lip at the tremor she heard in his voice. She turned in his arms and cupped his face in her hands. 'Same back at you.'

Nick pushed a strand of hair behind her ear. 'I'm glad we cleared the air. Now I know whether to accept your father's offer.'

'What offer?' Clem frowned. 'What does he have to do with it?'

Nick's naughty grin flashed. 'Well, when I asked him for your hand—'

Clem's mouth fell open. 'Seriously? You asked my father if you could marry me?'

'It seemed the right thing to do. Anyway, he said I was mad—'

'He did not!' Clem protested.

Nick sucked in his cheeks to keep from laughing '—and he offered me the choice between your mum's emerald engagement ring or writing off the balance of my loan.'

Clem's lips twitched. 'OK, let's pretend I believe that story... What did you tell him?'

'To write off the loan... What, are you nuts?'

'You're going to tease me for the rest of my life, aren't you?' Clem pinched the skin at his waist before sighing. 'I always wanted my mum's engagement ring as my own. My dad wouldn't have considered giving it to Cai.'

'Don't blame him, the guy is a moron.'

With one hand, Clem reached for her coffee and took a sip. 'If we get married, we'll have to book the entire Lodge for all our guests. When is the next date when the entire Lodge is empty?'

'Two years and six months,' Nick responded after giving it some thought. 'Can I at least take the ring and ask you if you'll marry me in two and a half years' time?'

'Mmm. You could do that. I might even say yes, depending on how romantic your proposal is,' Clem teased him back.

Nick's mouth twitched. 'You are such a princess.'

'Yes, but I'm your princess,' Clem said as she pushed her thumbs under the waistband of his shorts.

'Too right.'

'Nick?' she murmured. 'It really was an eland and you were just messing with me, weren't you?'

'No, it was a—' her hands moved '—it was anything you want it to be, sweetheart.'

Clem grinned. 'Much better,' she murmured against his mouth. 'Love you. Take me to bed.'

Nick picked her up and dumped her on the lounger. 'Too far. Right here, right now.' He rested his head between her breasts. 'You make me so damn happy, Red.'

Clem's heart thumped at the emotion in his voice and she pushed her hand through his hair. 'Me too and I plan for us to keep being happy for—at least—the next fifty years. That work for you?'

'Make it sixty and you've got a deal.'

EPILOGUE

Two years and eight months later...

Luella Dawson's final blog:

So, readers, I was one of the lucky people invited to Clem Copeland and Nick Sherwood's wedding at The Baobab and Buffalo Lodge in South Africa. Remember them? They had us enthralled a couple of years ago, watching them fall in love.

The bride and groom were married in a moonlight ceremony on Arthur's Hill in their game reserve. The bride wore a spectacular couture wedding dress and designer sandals, the groom wore a solid black tux and black wellington boots. (I asked but got some weird story about stepping on a snake...).

Their adorable eighteen-month-old son, Ross, wore the sweetest smile and sat on his father's hip the whole ceremony. And, as the African moon rose, they exchanged rings and promises to love, honour and protect each other...and their children. The one in their arms and—breaking news!—the one on the way.

I confess, I cried. Luckily, I was standing next to Clem's gorgeous father, Hugh, who happened to have a spare handkerchief and a broad shoulder. And a very naughty glint in his eye...

Have to say that those Full Moon picnics are very conducive to romance!

* * * * *

ROMANCE

Beholden to the Throne	Carol Marinelli
The Petrelli Heir	Kim Lawrence
Her Little White Lie	Maisey Yates
Her Shameful Secret	Susanna Carr
The Incorrigible Playboy	Emma Darcy
No Longer Forbidden?	Dani Collins
The Enigmatic Greek	Catherine George
The Night That Started It All	Anna Cleary
The Secret Wedding Dress	Ally Blake
Driving Her Crazy	Amy Andrews
The Heir's Proposal	Raye Morgan
The Soldier's Sweetheart	Soraya Lane
The Billionaire's Fair Lady	Barbara Wallace
A Bride for the Maverick Millionaire	Marion Lennox
Take One Arranged Marriage...	Shoma Narayanan
Wild About the Man	Joss Wood
Breaking the Playboy's Rules	Emily Forbes
Hot-Shot Doc Comes to Town	Susan Carlisle

MEDICAL

The Surgeon's Doorstep Baby	Marion Lennox
Dare She Dream of Forever?	Lucy Clark
Craving Her Soldier's Touch	Wendy S. Marcus
Secrets of a Shy Socialite	Wendy S. Marcus

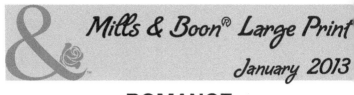

Mills & Boon® Large Print

January 2013

ROMANCE

Unlocking her Innocence	Lynne Graham
Santiago's Command	Kim Lawrence
His Reputation Precedes Him	Carole Mortimer
The Price of Retribution	Sara Craven
The Valtieri Baby	Caroline Anderson
Slow Dance with the Sheriff	Nikki Logan
Bella's Impossible Boss	Michelle Douglas
The Tycoon's Secret Daughter	Susan Meier
Just One Last Night	Helen Brooks
The Greek's Acquisition	Chantelle Shaw
The Husband She Never Knew	Kate Hewitt

HISTORICAL

His Mask of Retribution	Margaret McPhee
How to Disgrace a Lady	Bronwyn Scott
The Captain's Courtesan	Lucy Ashford
Man Behind the Façade	June Francis
The Highlander's Stolen Touch	Terri Brisbin

MEDICAL

Sydney Harbour Hospital: Marco's Temptation	Fiona McArthur
Waking Up With His Runaway Bride	Louisa George
The Legendary Playboy Surgeon	Alison Roberts
Falling for Her Impossible Boss	Alison Roberts
Letting Go With Dr Rodriguez	Fiona Lowe
Dr Tall, Dark...and Dangerous?	Lynne Marshall

1212 GEN STD LP

Mills & Boon® Hardback

February 2013

ROMANCE

Sold to the Enemy	Sarah Morgan
Uncovering the Silveri Secret	Melanie Milburne
Bartering Her Innocence	Trish Morey
Dealing Her Final Card	Jennie Lucas
In the Heat of the Spotlight	Kate Hewitt
No More Sweet Surrender	Caitlin Crews
Pride After Her Fall	Lucy Ellis
Living the Charade	Michelle Conder
The Downfall of a Good Girl	Kimberly Lang
The One That Got Away	Kelly Hunter
Her Rocky Mountain Protector	Patricia Thayer
The Billionaire's Baby SOS	Susan Meier
Baby out of the Blue	Rebecca Winters
Ballroom to Bride and Groom	Kate Hardy
How To Get Over Your Ex	Nikki Logan
Must Like Kids	Jackie Braun
The Brooding Doc's Redemption	Kate Hardy
The Son that Changed his Life	Jennifer Taylor

MEDICAL

An Inescapable Temptation	Scarlet Wilson
Revealing The Real Dr Robinson	Dianne Drake
The Rebel and Miss Jones	Annie Claydon
Swallowbrook's Wedding of the Year	Abigail Gordon

EN STD HB

Mills & Boon® Large Print

February 2013

ROMANCE

Banished to the Harem	Carol Marinelli
Not Just the Greek's Wife	Lucy Monroe
A Delicious Deception	Elizabeth Power
Painted the Other Woman	Julia James
Taming the Brooding Cattleman	Marion Lennox
The Rancher's Unexpected Family	Myrna Mackenzie
Nanny for the Millionaire's Twins	Susan Meier
Truth-Or-Date.com	Nina Harrington
A Game of Vows	Maisey Yates
A Devil in Disguise	Caitlin Crews
Revelations of the Night Before	Lynn Raye Harris

HISTORICAL

Two Wrongs Make a Marriage	Christine Merrill
How to Ruin a Reputation	Bronwyn Scott
When Marrying a Duke...	Helen Dickson
No Occupation for a Lady	Gail Whitiker
Tarnished Rose of the Court	Amanda McCabe

MEDICAL

Sydney Harbour Hospital: Ava's Re-Awakening	Carol Marinelli
How To Mend A Broken Heart	Amy Andrews
Falling for Dr Fearless	Lucy Clark
The Nurse He Shouldn't Notice	Susan Carlisle
Every Boy's Dream Dad	Sue MacKay
Return of the Rebel Surgeon	Connie Cox

Discover Pure Reading Pleasure with

MILLS
BOON®
™

Visit the Mills & Boon website for all the latest in romance

Buy all the latest releases, backlist and eBooks

Find out more about our authors and their books

Join our community and chat to authors and other readers

Free online reads from your favourite authors

Win with our fantastic online competitions

Sign up for our free monthly eNewsletter

Tell us what you think by signing up to our reader panel

Rate and review books with our star system

www.millsandboon.co.uk

 Follow us at twitter.com/millsandboonuk

 Become a fan at facebook.com/romancehq